"Stop fighting it," he whispered

"You know you want me as much as I want you, Laura. Your mouth told me that when I kissed you the last time you were here. Your whole body told me—desire came off your skin, a heat I could feel with my fingertips..."

She was hot now, face burning, body burning. But she wouldn't give in, either to him or to her own incomprehensible emotions.

"I'm never going to let you go away again, Laura," he said in a deep, harsh voice, and then he lowered his body against her....

CHARLOTTE LAMB is one of Harlequin's best-loved and bestselling authors. Born in the East End of London, Charlotte spent her early childhood moving from relative to relative to escape the bombings of World War II. After working as a secretary in the BBC's European department, she married a political reporter who wrote for *The Times*. Charlotte recalls that it was at his suggestion that she began to write, "because it was one job I could do without having to leave our five children." Charlotte and her family now live in a beautiful home on the Isle of Man. It is the perfect setting for an author who creates characters and stories that have helped shape the face of romance fiction around the world.

Books by Charlotte Lamb

HARLEQUIN PRESENTS PLUS
1560—SLEEPING PARTNERS
1584—FORBIDDEN FRUIT

HARLEQUIN PRESENTS: BARBARY WHARF
1498—BESIEGED
1509—BATTLE FOR POSSESSION
1513—TOO CLOSE FOR COMFORT
1522—PLAYING HARD TO GET
1530—A SWEET ADDICTION
1540—SURRENDER

HARLEQUIN PRESENTS
1618—DREAMING
1658—FIRE IN THE BLOOD

Charlotte Lamb

FALLING IN LOVE

Harlequin Books

TORONTO • NEW YORK • LONDON
AMSTERDAM • PARIS • SYDNEY • HAMBURG
STOCKHOLM • ATHENS • TOKYO • MILAN
MADRID • WARSAW • BUDAPEST • AUCKLAND

ISBN 0-373-11672-1

FALLING IN LOVE

CHAPTER ONE

THE March day had begun with showers and cool weather, but as Patrick Ogilvie walked across the bridge into the centre of York the sun came out and the air suddenly smelt of spring. He was about to walk into Laura's office when he realised that the sweet scent came from the buckets of flowers standing on the pavement outside a florist's shop across the street. On impulse he ran across and bought an armful: fragile white narcissi, great yellow daffodils and spears of deep blue hyacinth, their fragrance so strong that when he walked into the office block the receptionist in the lobby stared and sighed.

'Oh...aren't they lovely? Now I know it's spring!'

He pulled a few of the flowers out of the armful and offered them to her, smiling.

'I wasn't hinting...' she said, looking pink and startled, which secretly amused Patrick, who hadn't expected to get such a reaction from her. Julia Wood wasn't a girl, after all; she was a woman in her early thirties, dark and serious, with a warmly rounded figure. Julia had had to come back to work after years out of the workforce, because her husband had died young of a heart attack, leaving her with two children aged twelve and ten. At first she had been very shy and nervous, but she had

been working here for six months now and Patrick
had been fascinated to watch her self-confidence
grow.

'I know you weren't hinting, Julia,' he half
teased. 'I've got masses of them here, take them!
And don't forget to put them into water before they
wilt, will you?'

She took the flowers, looking down at them with
a dreamy little smile, but said anxiously, 'I hope
Miss Grainger won't be cross when she hears you
gave me some of her flowers, though! Is it her
birthday?'

He shook his head. 'No, that's in July. I bought
these because they meant spring had really started,
and it's been such a long winter. She won't mind
at all. In fact, I should have thought of it before—
you ought to have flowers on your desk, it would
make a good impression.'

Julia beamed. 'Oh, that would be lovely. I think
it would look good! Thanks, Patrick, you've made
my day.'

He nodded. 'Not at all. I won't forget to mention
it to her. It will be just the touch to make the clients
feel welcome.'

He walked away, towards the lift, and Julia
watched him a little wistfully. Just now he had reminded her of her husband: the quick smile, the
kind gesture, the warmth. John had had all those;
they were what she missed most—the little gestures
which had made their life together such a happy
one. Of course, he hadn't been as good-looking as
Patrick Ogilvie, not that that had mattered to her.
She had loved the way he looked: his direct blue

eyes and happy grin, his floppy brown hair, broad shoulders and the way he ...

She broke off, eyes brimming, got up and fumbled to pick up the flowers Patrick had given her, her head bent to hide her face.

'Fred, will you watch my desk? I've just got to put these in water,' she said huskily as she ran to the cloakroom, just in time before the tears came.

Laura's secretary, Anne, was working intently when Patrick walked into her office, but she broke off, looking up, her face lighting up at the sight of him. Women always smiled at Patrick like that; he was not merely accustomed to it, he expected it and would have missed it if he didn't get those bright-eyed glances.

'Good morning, Anne, how are you?' Patrick asked as if he really cared, which he did. He liked people and it made him happy to know that all was well with them. If Patrick had a flaw it was that he preferred life on the sunny side and tended to avoid anyone who might depress him.

Anne never did. She told him gaily that she was fine, how was he?

'Great,' he said. 'Is anyone with her?' he added, looking at the door on the left which led into Laura's office.

Anne shook her head. 'No, but don't go in yet— she's talking on the phone and said she wasn't to be disturbed.'

Patrick shrugged amiably, and took a seat on the edge of Anne's desk. 'You look very pretty today— new dress?' he asked, running his blue gaze over her. 'That colour is perfect for you; you should wear it more often.'

Anne's flush deepened; she looked down, smoothing a hand over the pink wool dress, suddenly aware, under his gaze, that the way it clung to her breasts and hips made her thin body look far more feminine and that the colour warmed her sallow skin.

'Thank you, Patrick.' It was typical of him to notice and to comment; she secretly glanced at him through her lashes, sighing. If only he weren't in love with Laura Grainger! Or if only she worked for him and could see him every day. That would be heaven.

She had been half in love with Patrick Ogilvie from the first time he walked into the office, but with Laura Grainger around Anne knew he would never look at anyone else. No man would. Laura Grainger was a knock-out: the sort of blonde men dreamt about. Popular myth had it that blondes were dumb. Not Laura. She was not only clever, she was street-smart, too. A devastating combination. No wonder she had been so successful at her job. Anne knew she would never get as far in the public relations field as Laura Grainger had—she was neither street-smart nor brainy—but she didn't envy her boss's success in work half as much as she coveted her boyfriend.

Anne had always loved tall men, and Patrick was a good six feet, not a spare ounce of flesh on him, with smooth dark brown hair and a charm that surely only a stone-hearted woman could resist.

Anne couldn't, anyway, especially when his face had that little-boy look it sometimes wore.

Every woman in the office block was crazy about Patrick Ogilvie, in fact. With all the attention and fuss he got, it wouldn't have been surprising if he had been totally spoilt and selfish, but that was the most amazing thing about him. Patrick was warm-hearted, caring, kind and endlessly thoughtful. When Laura was busy, he did her shopping for her. Sometimes he even tidied up her flat and often cooked her meals. There was nothing he wouldn't do for her.

Anne liked her boss, but sometimes she wished Laura Grainger didn't exist. Maybe then Patrick might look her way?

A buzz made Anne jump. Hurriedly, she flicked down a switch on the console of her desk. 'Yes, Laura?'

'I've finished my phone call, Anne,' Laura Grainger's clear, cool voice said. 'Any messages?'

'No, but——'

Laura didn't give her a chance to finish that sentence. 'I wonder why I haven't heard from Barry yet? Oh, well, before I forget, Anne, I have to see Mr Eyre on Tuesday, ten o'clock. I'll probably be there all morning and it might stretch into lunch. If I have another appointment, make sure it's shifted to some other time, would you?'

'Yes, of course. Laura, Patrick is here,' Anne said, scribbling hurriedly on her pad with a frantic air.

'Send him in, then get the Courtleys Agency on the line for me, will you?' Laura's voice was businesslike and didn't alter at the news that Patrick was there. How could she be so casual when the mere mention of his name made Anne's heart leap like a salmon fighting its way upstream?

Anne's brown eyes wistfully watched Patrick depart, his long legs moving gracefully and fast, as though he couldn't wait to see Laura. He didn't even look back. Anne sighed, then the phone rang and she picked it up.

'Dudley and Grainger Public Relations, Miss Grainger's office. Mr Dale? Oh, yes. I'll see if Miss Grainger is free to talk to you.'

Patrick was walking towards her desk when the phone rang and Laura automatically picked it up, flicking a look at him, her green eyes smiling, and mouthed 'Hi!' before saying aloud, 'Who? Mr Dale? Yes, put him through. Hello, Mr Dale—have you found anything interesting for me?'

Patrick opened his arms and let spring flowers tumble down all over her desk; their scent by now had been intensified by the central heating in the building and it filled the room with the fragrance of spring.

Laura looked down, startled, looked up again, her wide mouth curling in soundless laughter, and blew him a silent kiss.

'Yes, quite right,' she said into the phone.

Patrick walked round her desk, picking up a narcissus as he did so. He stood behind her, his slim body leaning on the back of her chair, and began stroking her clear-skinned face with the flower.

She gave a stifled snort of laughter.

'Stop it! That tickles!' she whispered, covering the mouthpiece of the phone with her hand, pushing the narcissus away and then speaking into the phone. 'No, I haven't had time to look at what you sent me, Mr Dale. I've been too busy, but I'll get round to it this evening.'

Patrick let the flower trail lightly down her chin to her throat, leaving a faint trace of golden pollen on her pale skin. When he began to stroke her breasts with it, his breathing quickening, Laura captured the narcissus and removed it from him, still talking calmly on the phone.

'Yes, that's exactly what I've been looking for! When can I see it?'

Patrick gave an audible sigh and sat back on the edge of her desk, watching her profile, half wryly, half with passion. Her pale gold hair shone in the spring sunlight, a light, wild mass of curls framing her elegant, fine-boned face. Sometimes he wondered if he would ever see her eyes light up with the same passion he felt for her.

'This afternoon?' Laura said, frowning. She was very aware of the way Patrick was looking at her and knew him far too well not to know what he was thinking. She shouldn't have stopped him touching her, just now; he had that hurt look in his eyes and Laura hated to feel she'd hurt him. 'No,' she said absently. 'That isn't possible, I'm afraid. Any time during the weekend would suit me better. Tomorrow? Yes, eleven o'clock, Saturday, at your office, then; thank you, Mr Dale.'

She hung up and turned to Patrick, her eyes a vivid green in the sunlight. 'That was Dale, the estate agent; he says a new place just came on to the market, just what we want. Can you come on Saturday morning? We could see this cottage, then have lunch somewhere in the country.'

'Good idea.' Patrick nodded, brightening. 'Where is this cottage? Far from York?'

'Quite a drive, apparently, and it's not a straight run. That's why we're meeting Mr Dale at his office in Malton; he'll show us the way there, and take us over the cottage. He said you drive from Malton as if you were going back to York, then take the Castle Howard road, and it's six or so miles further on from Castle Howard itself, right out in the country. It was a farm cottage once. It's isolated— some miles from the nearest village—but the farm is just across a field, Mr Dale said.'

Patrick looked a little dubious. 'Do we want somewhere that isolated? Is there a road to this cottage, or is it in the middle of a field? Why do I get the feeling that I'm going to have to drive miles every day to get milk and bread?'

'If the farm is that close, we'll be able to get our milk and eggs fresh every day, and no doubt we could buy other things from them.'

'Did Mr Dale tell you the price?'

'A little below our maximum figure!' said Laura triumphantly, and he made a disbelieving noise.

'Well, that's a first! All the others Dale suggested were above our maximum.'

'Exactly. But we've been disappointed too often—I'm not getting too excited until I see it.' She absently glanced down at the spring flowers on her desk and began to laugh, throwing back her head. 'What on earth do you think you're doing, buying all those flowers, you crazy man? What am I supposed to do with them all?' She bent her head to inhale their fragrance and her blonde hair fell in ringlets and coils all over her face. 'Mmm... gorgeous; you do think of the nicest presents! I love them!'

'Never mind them—how about me? You're supposed to tell me that you love me!'

'I don't need to; you already know I do!' Laura said, green eyes looking at him through her long hair.

He pushed the hair back from her face to kiss her. 'I'm so crazy about you,' he whispered passionately against her mouth, and his hand ran up her spine, pressing her closer, his body touching her.

Laura kissed him back, gently, clasping his face between her palms, but when his caresses became more heated she pulled back, rather flushed. 'Not in the office, Patrick!' she muttered. 'If a client walked in it could be embarrassing!'

Patrick gave a little grimace. 'I know, sorry, but... you go to my head. OK, shall we go to lunch?'

She gave him an apologetic look. 'Darling, I'm sorry, but——'

'Laura, we had a date—I've booked for lunch at the Apollo!'

'I know, and I'm sorry,' Laura said ruefully. 'I just can't spare the time. I have to talk to the agency and fix a shoot with these girls for next week and then talk to the photographer again. There's been

a lot to do today. Look, let's ring up and cancel
the table and eat lunch up here. I'll send out for
sandwiches and fruit and some coffee.' She kissed
him on the nose, hugging him. 'And I'll sit on your
knee while we wait, how's that?'

'I see! Bribery and corruption,' he said, laughing
and relaxing again. 'Sounds good to me, although
I can think of something I'd like even better.'

'Don't you ever think of anything else?' she
asked, half exasperated, half amused.

'Don't you ever think of it at all?' Patrick muttered, and wasn't really joking; a silence fell between them and Laura gave him a stricken look.

'Patrick! You know I love you! It's just that I'm
not as . . . well . . . I suppose as highly sexed as you
are . . . Sex isn't on my mind all day.'

'It's on mine whenever I see you,' he said,
huskily, sending a wave of regret through her.

'Oh . . . I'm sorry, darling—if I——'

Anne buzzed her at that second. 'I've got the
agency on the line for you now,' her voice said
tinnily, and Laura couldn't quite suppress a sigh of
relief.

'Right. Put them through, then go down to the
snack bar across the street and get us sandwiches,
fruit, and cans of diet cola out of the fridge. Then
you can go to lunch.'

Patrick listened and watched her, his mouth wry.
Sometimes he was jealous of her job, of this firm.
Sometimes he felt afraid, suspecting that the job
meant more to her than he did, got far more of her
attention. His own work meant a lot to him, but
Laura mattered ten times more. Since they'd first

met she had filled his life until nothing else meant
much to him. He wished she felt the same about
him, but sensed that she didn't. There was some
sort of irony in that for Patrick, who had all his
life been able to bowl women over and make them
his devoted slaves.

He was twenty-nine, and until he'd met Laura
he had had a wonderful time with a constantly
changing succession of pretty girls. He had liked
them all, but never fallen in love with any of them.
Why, when he did fall in love, had he fallen like a
ton of bricks for someone who was so cool and in
command of herself? At times he almost felt Laura
treated him more as a brother than a lover. Oh, she
was affectionate, loving, almost indulgent with him,
but the passion he felt for her was never reflected
in her eyes when she looked back at him.

He wished she would agree to fix a date for their
wedding. Once they were married he might feel
more secure. He might stop being scared she would
meet someone else.

The following morning Patrick woke up late, with
all the symptoms of flu. He was shivering, his throat
hurt and his head ached. After taking aspirin and
deciding to skip breakfast, since his appetite had
vanished, he gloomily rang Laura.

'Oh, poor darling,' she said with instant sympathy. 'Shall I come round?'

'Better not,' he croaked. 'Don't want you to catch
it. But it means I shan't be able to come
to see the cottage.'

'Never mind, I'll go, and report back to you later. Sure you don't want me to come and hold your hand when I get back?'

He laughed hoarsely. 'I'd love it, but I'll probably sleep all day; I'm having trouble keeping awake.'

'Best thing for you!' she agreed. 'Look after yourself, take plenty of liquids, and stay warm.'

She rang off after blowing him a kiss and ruefully looked out of the window. Typical. The weather was glorious, wouldn't you know it? They could have had such a wonderful day. She took another look at the cloudless blue sky. Well, it would still be a very pleasant drive; far better to be out in the countryside on a day like this, instead of sitting around in an office!

Laura lived in a small apartment on the fifth floor of a modern block of flats a short walk from York Castle. She had a good view of the river from her sitting-room window. Her tiny bedroom looked out over roof-tops but gave her a glimpse of the world-famous medieval Minster.

She liked uncluttered rooms, with lots of space, so there was a minimum of furniture—only what she really liked and felt she needed. Most of it had been bought in antique shops or at sales over the years she had lived there, or had been given to her by a relative. Laura preferred to live with graceful old furniture which had been well loved for years before she owned it. Fortunately, she had generous relatives, most of them living in Yorkshire. Hers was a very close family; she saw them all often: her parents, who lived in a tiny village fifty miles away, her married sister in Harrogate, or one or other of her grandparents. Sometimes they came to York to visit her, especially her parents, who loved their visits to the city.

Laura always put them up in her flat, insisting on giving them the bedroom while she slept in her sitting-room on a couch, and she took them out to restaurants, to the theatre or a cinema. It gave her pleasure to see them enjoying themselves, but she knew that they were happy to get home again, back to the village where they had lived all their lives.

Laura missed the village, too, and the moorland landscape she remembered waking up to each morning. When she had inherited a large sum of money from an uncle a year or so back, she had decided to buy a cottage within easy driving distance of York so that she could spend weekends in the countryside. Of course, the landscape would be different—softer, less rugged than the one she had grown up with—but she wanted to hear birds singing, escape the everlasting sound of traffic and the smell of petrol fumes, go for Sunday morning walks across fields, through woods.

When she and Patrick had got engaged, he'd been delighted with the idea of a country home after they were married, because he was tired of living in the city, too, but since he worked from home, as a free-lance artist, he wouldn't be driving to York and back each day, and somewhere in the real countryside would also suit him better. He would sell his flat, and live entirely in the country, but Laura had decided to keep hers. It would be more convenient for her to live in York during the working week and her family would still be able to make their occasional visits to the city.

'I can do any redecorating necessary. I prefer to do it myself—most decorators don't have any taste,' Patrick had predictably said.

'That will save us money,' she had agreed, and had been teased for her Yorkshire sense of thrift. 'Well,' she had defiantly retorted, 'that's how I was brought up! To count the pennies. You wouldn't want a wife who chucks money around, would you?'

'Certainly wouldn't,' he had grinned, then said, 'Oh, it will be fun, Laura! During the week, in between doing my work, I'll have lots to do around the house and garden, so I won't be lonely, or miss you too much, and then at weekends we can make love and talk by the fire or in the garden! We're going to have a wonderful life.'

Whenever Laura met old girlfriends she was usually appalled by the men they had picked. Most of them had husbands who, however attractive or pleasant they might seem, were stuck in the conventional male path—spoilt, thoughtless, domineering, expecting to be waited on hand and foot, to have a well-cooked meal on the table when they came home from work, their perfectly laundered shirts hanging in the wardrobe ready for them to put on each morning.

Her friends were always complaining about them. Yet they stayed with them, almost seemed proud of their behaviour. Laura found it baffling. Thank heavens Patrick wasn't like that. He was a partner, not a master: good-looking, charming, but kind-hearted and easygoing too. He had a delightful personality and Laura had never met anyone, male or female, who didn't like him, but he was also intensely practical and hard-working. He could cook better than she could, he loved to see his home looking spotless and spent hours every week doing housework, doing his own washing, ironing, even sewing on buttons if he lost one from a shirt.

She suddenly caught sight of a clock on a table; good heavens, was that the time? She ought to be on her way; traffic coming into York would be quite heavy soon.

She paused at the front door to check her reflection in the mirror hanging there. Her blonde hair was a tossing cloud of curls, her skin was smooth and dewy, her full mouth softly pink—but it was on her slanting green eyes that her stare stayed. Why was there that look in them? She couldn't even define it, but she didn't look like a rapturously happy woman, and she ought to! Life was showering her with everything she had ever wanted, so why did she feel so restless?

But she knew why! Patrick was everything she wanted a man to be, and yet...and yet she had never once felt the sort of overwhelming desire for him that she knew he felt for her.

Well, so what? she defiantly told her reflection. Did you have to feel like that to be in love? That might be one aspect of love, but it wasn't everything. But her green eyes silently held the answer: isn't it? Why did she feel this restless, unsatisfied need if it wasn't important?

Is there something wrong with me? Why don't I want Patrick the way he wants me? When he made love to her she always felt a sensual enjoyment, pleasure in the stroking hands and warm mouth, the gentle physical contact, but she had never once gone crazy, lost her head, ached for him, and it disturbed her. She knew it disturbed Patrick, too; and it hurt her to know she was hurting him, because she loved him. But was loving him enough?

If only she dared talk to her sister, or had a friend she trusted enough to ask, Am I just cold by nature? I'm not frigid, am I? What is the matter with me?

But maybe she had let herself get wound up over nothing; maybe she would change after she and Patrick were married, when they were alone all weekend in their cottage and the tensions of their engagement were over?

The telephone rang; she ran to pick it up. 'Hello? Laura Grainger speaking.'

'Laura, we've got a crisis!' It was Barry Courtley's voice, sounding agitated.

'What now?' she demanded, instantly alert. Why did she go on working with his model agency? He seemed to rush from one crisis to another; he was the most disorganised man! He could definitely learn a thing or two from Patrick!

'The shoot at Castle Howard!' panted Barry.

'What about it?'

'The girls will finish there at eleven-thirty and have to be back in York by twelve-thirty to start shooting in the Shambles by one, but their driver has broken down on the road and I can't get another taxi out there in time. Saturday is always a busy day for them.'

'Haven't any of the girls got a car, for heaven's sake? Why did you have to lay on a taxi?'

'It's safer,' mumbled Barry. 'Then they can't plead they got stuck in traffic or their car wouldn't start. The taxi goes round and picks them all up, drops them at wherever they're shooting, then goes back for them...only this time the taxi broke down *en route* and there isn't another free for ages.'

'What about the photographer?'

'He only has a small two-seater van; his equipment takes up most of the space in the back, and he has that hulking great assistant in the front with him. I'd go myself, but I'm due at my sister's wedding in Durham at three; I've got to leave right away, then I thought of you...'

'Oh, did you?' she retorted. 'I'm busy too, Barry! I've got better things to do with my time than play chauffeur to your girls!'

'But you did say you were going that way this morning and might look in on the Castle Howard shoot!' he protested, wounded innocence in his tones.

Laura had to admit that. Still frowning, she did some quick calculations. 'Yes, OK, I'll pick them up. How many girls was it? Four? Yes, I can just about squeeze them into my Mini. I have to be at Malton by eleven, and should be at Castle Howard at around eleven-thirty. The timing will be tight— I have to see a cottage—but supposing that we leave there at twelve...yes, I can do it. Will you be able to talk to the girls first?'

'Yes, they're going to ring me back.'

'Well, tell them to meet me at the main gate, at eleven-thirty. Will they have much stuff with them?'

'Clothes, make-up, shoes, the usual stuff. They might be able to stow some of that in the photographer's van, if it helps.'

'Well, I should have room in my car. Now, I'd better go or I'll be late too.'

The drive to Malton was quite a rapid run, in spite of the traffic going from and coming to York, and she reached the estate agent's office exactly on time. As she pulled up outside, the estate agent emerged, smiling.

Mr Dale was a broad, short Yorkshire man with a face like a well-weathered prune. He shook hands with a firm grip, giving her the grimace which passed for a smile with him.

'Well, I think we've finally come up with exactly what you've been wanting, Miss Grainger. Nice little property, needs the odd job done to it, mind—lick of paint, some work on the roof—but it could be made very comfortable without costing an arm and a leg. It's not an easy trip from here; do you want to come with me, or will you take your own car?'

'I'll take my own car, then I can drive straight back to York,' she decided, and he nodded.

'Follow me close, then, Miss Grainger; don't get yourself lost. Remember, we're turning off at the Castle Howard road.'

He was about to climb into his car, but she stopped him. 'Mr Dale, I have to pick some girls up from Castle Howard on our way. It won't take a minute; they should be waiting for us at the main gates.'

'Work there, do they?' he asked, looking interested.

'No, they're models; they've been working in the grounds, with a photographer.'

The drive back towards York was easier because the roads were not quite so crowded now. The road which led to Castle Howard had once been the private road of the family who owned the castle; they had built it in the days long before cars. About seven miles long, it ran across country, between green fields, and wasn't busy, so they were able to drive fast. It was just after half-past eleven when they arrived at Castle Howard's main gate, and to Laura's relief the girls were waiting as arranged.

'This is ace of you, Laura,' a skinny black-haired girl said, clambering in beside her, folding her long, long legs somehow into the limited space available. The other girls climbed into the back and settled themselves, pushing and giggling.

Mr Dale had drawn up in front of Laura's car and was waiting, watching in his driving mirror as the models one by one vanished into the little Mini. Laura could see his bemused expression in his mirror.

'Thought we were going to have to walk!' one of the girls in the back said. 'Thanks, Laura.'

'That's OK, I was passing the gates anyway. All in? Then off we go.' Laura waved to Mr Dale, who started his engine again and moved away with her car following him.

'Barry's such a skinflint,' the black-haired girl said crossly. 'He always books the cheapest transport—he gets block bookings for half the price and they send their oldest car or coach, and it's always breaking down. I'm fed up with him—I'm moving to another agency down south as soon as I can get placed.'

The girls in the back made mocking noises. One of them drawled, 'That'll be the day! You've been saying that for as long as I can remember, Suzy.'

'I mean it this time!'

'Sure you do!' the other girls drawled, and her friends in the back seat giggled.

'It's like driving around with a lot of kids; stop squabbling,' Laura said, then ruefully realised that kids were what most of them were. Suzy was twenty-one now, Yasmin nineteen, but the others were mostly sixteen or seventeen.

Mr Dale had turned off the road now on to a rough, bumpy track between wire fences which clearly led eventually to a farm. Laura followed him; the car bumped and grated over ruts in the track. Laura hated to think what this was doing to her tyres. Surely this wasn't the only road to this cottage?

Then she saw it and her green eyes widened, glowing. In one glance she saw that it was the sort of place she had always dreamt of living in. An old flint and stone-built cottage with a slate roof, set in a walled garden with an apple tree leaning over the gate, it stood alone with fields all round it, and Laura loved it at sight.

She pulled up behind Mr Dale's car and got out, slamming her door. The models fell out, chattering excitedly.

'Oh, isn't it sweet? You going to buy it, Laura?' Yasmin asked, walking with difficulty on the rough surface of the track in her stilt-like heels.

'Is this where you and Patrick are going to live when you're married?' asked Suzy.

'Oh, he's lovely,' cooed Yasmin. 'You are lucky, Laura. Mind if we gatecrash the church? I'd love to see you getting married.'

'I'll send you an invitation,' promised Laura, and the other girls excitedly chattered to her.

'For all of us? Can we all come to the wedding? Oh, great, thanks, Laura.'

'Want a bridesmaid?' Yasmin asked wistfully. 'I've never been a real bridesmaid. I dressed up as one, once, for that bridal shop advert—ever so pretty the dress was, sort of peach satin, lots of lace, too, and I carried a little round bouquet of creamy rosebuds with a silver foil backing. I kept it afterwards, got it hanging on my dressing-table; it dried lovely, the roses still smell nice. But I've never been a real bridesmaid.'

Two girls were tottering along the track, giggling. 'Ooh, look, there's cows in this field...black and white ones! Moo, moo, come here, moos! Look at them staring; what a hoot... I've never seen one this close, have you, Yaz? Come and look! Haven't they got big heads...oh, look at that one's tongue—all rough, like sandpaper... Hello, moos...'

Mr Dale watched them with a mixture of disbelief and indulgence. 'No brains at all, have they?' he murmured to Laura, who smiled and shrugged.

'They're nice girls, though, when you get to know them.'

At that instant a tractor turned out of one of the fields and chugged noisily towards them only to stop dead, the engine throbbing, while the driver stared at them with a dark scowl on his face.

He shouted something Laura couldn't hear above the noise of his tractor, and waved his arms at them.

Mr Dale groaned.

'What did he say?' asked Laura, but before the estate agent could answer the tractor driver switched off his engine and shouted again, and this time they all heard what he said.

'How many times do I have to tell you? Get off my land or I'll set my dogs on you!'

The models shrieked and ran back towards the car.

'His land?' Laura asked Mr Dale. 'I don't understand; is this his cottage?'

'No, no, it belongs to a lady who's lived here for years.'

'Then what does he mean, his land?'

Mr Dale didn't answer. He was looking nervous. The tractor driver had jumped down, was striding towards them, long, muscled legs rapidly covering the ground. Laura tensed with an instant hostility. He was everything she disliked in a man. Tall, broad, with thick, windswept black hair, he certainly couldn't be accused of charm or good looks. His face rugged, powerful, he had a jaw she recognised as belligerent, even at a distance, and piercing grey eyes glittering with rage.

'Ooh . . .' giggled the models, clustering behind Laura, as if for protection. 'He looks real mad, doesn't he? Wouldn't want to meet him on a dark night.'

'Don't know about that! Wouldn't mind at all, actually!' Yasmin whispered and set them all shrieking with laughter, which didn't soften the lines of the man's angry face.

'Who is he?' Laura hurriedly asked Mr Dale, who crossly muttered back,

'Josh Kern. He owns the farm, all this land . . .' His voice broke off as the dark man reached them and stopped, his legs apart in a threatening stance.

Mr Dale was not the nervous type, but Laura saw his throat move convulsively as he swallowed.

'For the last time, will you get off my land?' snarled Josh Kern.

Mr Dale stood his ground, facing up to him. 'Mr Kern, you don't own this cottage, and the owner has been using this right of way for many years, as you know perfectly well.'

'There's no right of way; this is a private road, and I'm taking legal steps to establish that fact!' Josh Kern snarled. 'Now, get these women out of here, and don't come back!'

Laura bristled. 'I came here to see this cottage, Mr Kern, and as you don't own it you can't stop me!'

He slowly swung his head in her direction, his grey eyes full of menace.

'Don't be so sure about that, whoever you are.'

'She's Laura Grainger,' Yasmin told him, her face flushed with the excitement of the conflict, and determined to get his attention. She wasn't frightened. In fact, this was her idea of fun, watching an angry man bellowing at someone, especially a man this sexy. It beat hanging around waiting to be photographed any day!

She was disappointed, however. Josh Kern ignored her. He went on staring narrowly at Laura, from her clouds of blonde curls and full pink mouth to her long, slender legs and tiny feet, his cold eyes contemptuous.

'Who are all these people, Dale? Actresses?' he bit out, flicking a glance over the other girls with the same distaste.

'Models,' Mr Dale growled.

Josh Kern's mouth tightened. 'Models!'

The girls posed for him, smiles inviting.

His face tightened. 'My God! Are they all planning to move in here? Not if I can stop it. Listen to me, Miss ... whatever your name is ... if you're the one who might buy this place ... Did Mr Dale explain that this cottage really belongs to my farm? That it was given to someone, not sold, and that I want it back? I hoped to get it back legally, because there was no legal conveyance, just a scribbled paper saying the cottage was a gift, but the court upheld it. Then I tried to buy it back, but my offer was refused although it was far more than the cottage is worth on the open market. The present owner insists she'll only sell to someone else. Anyone else, so long as it isn't me, apparently!'

His eyes flashed. 'Apparently, I can't force her to sell it back to me...'

Clearly, thought Laura, he wished he could!

He went on fiercely, 'But I can refuse to let anyone who buys the place use my land as an access road, so be warned! If you do buy Fern Cottage you'll be buying yourself a lot of trouble.'

'Don't you threaten me!' Laura bit back at him, her head up and her green eyes very angry.

'I'm not threatening, I'm warning,' Josh Kern said very softly, and something in that dark face made her skin turn cold.

The other girls gazed, transfixed, their eyes wide and incredulous.

Laura knew how they felt; this man was not someone you could ignore or forget. He had such penetrating eyes; in his rage they turned silvery, as though white-hot.

Mr Dale cleared his throat and nervously suggested, 'Shall we go and look round the cottage now, Miss Grainger?'

'Yes,' she murmured, her eyes still held by Josh Kern's menacing stare.

'I meant every word,' he said in that soft, dangerous voice, and she believed him. He had the look of a man who always meant what he said.

Maybe she should forget any idea of buying Fern Cottage?

CHAPTER TWO

'HE CAN'T do anything to stop us using his road!
If someone lived in that cottage for years and used
his road all that time then that makes it a legal right
of way,' Patrick said on the phone later that day
when Laura rang him to report on the cottage.

'That's what Mr Dale said. He told me to ignore
the threats; there was no way we could be denied
access if we bought the cottage.'

'Mind you,' Patrick said thoughtfully, 'this
farmer chap... what did you say his name was?'

'Josh Kern,' said Laura, investing the name with
scorn.

Patrick gave a hoarse crow of amusement. 'Josh
Kern! How could I forget that? But seriously,
darling, he could make life rather awkward,
couldn't he? I wonder if it's worth it to go ahead?
Do we want to find ourselves in the middle of a
war with our neighbours?'

'I'm not being frightened off by some hulking
great brute of a farmer huffing and puffing at me!'

'I can't imagine you being scared, even by a
hulking great brute.' Patrick laughed, then more
seriously added, 'I'm sorry I wasn't there to take
him on, darling. Damn this flu; why do illnesses
always come at such inconvenient times? From what
you say about the cottage it's just what we were
looking for, and the price is way below what we

would have expected. We should have guessed there would be snags. What did you say to Dale?'

'That you'd have to see the cottage before we could give him a decision, so we have time to think about it. I'm glad your headache's better, even if your throat sounds worse. Shall I come round tomorrow morning and cook you some lunch?'

'I don't want you to catch this, Laura. Better not come over. I'm not hungry, anyway. I'm drinking lots of fruit juice and I ate an orange just now. I've got plenty of eggs and cheese; I can always whip up an omelette if I do get hungry.'

Wryly, she said, 'And your omelettes are ten times better than mine! In fact, anything you cook is ten times better.'

He laughed, but didn't deny it. Instead he yawned, then said, 'Sorry, darling... I've been sleeping on and off all day, but I still seem very tired.'

'Then I'll let you get back to sleep,' she said. 'Get well soon; I miss you.'

She put the phone down and stared out of the window at the busy York street below. Yes, it was a pity Patrick hadn't been with her. Maybe then that man wouldn't have talked to her, looked at her, the way he had. Her face ran with scarlet, remembering Josh Kern's contemptuous eyes as he'd looked her up and down. She could never remember meeting anyone she disliked more; it had been like running into a stone wall. Her whole body still ached with the shock of it.

'Who does he think he is?' she had demanded of Mr Dale after Josh Kern had climbed back on to his tractor and driven away.

'He knows who he is! He's Josh Kern of Kern House, and he owns all this,' Mr Dale had said drily, waving an arm around in a circle. 'Four hundred acres of good farm land, half arable; last year he had a fairish crop of barley, but he runs stock, too. A good dairy herd—Friesians. He's starting to run sheep on the hill up there too now, I gather. That's new. His father never had sheep, never did much with that land, except a bit of rough shooting. Plenty of rabbits and some game birds up there—I've shot with him in the past. Not much use for anything else, that land, old Jack Kern always said; not worth clearing the gorse and heather, but upland sheep can live on very little. Josh Kern's a canny chap; he's done some controlled burning up there, rid the land of most of the scrub, and ploughed it up.'

Mr Dale looked respectfully and wryly after the farmer, who was disappearing into another field. 'Aye, Josh works like a demon himself, and he gets good work out of his men—he expects his land to work, too.'

'If you ask me, he expects too much!' Laura muttered, still angry after the encounter with Josh Kern. 'And he isn't threatening me and getting away with it!'

'Good for you, then,' said Mr Dale, looking rather relieved. 'I was hoping you wouldn't let Josh scare you away.'

Her eyes narrowed. 'Has he scared many would-be buyers away?'

Mr Dale didn't answer. He pretended not to hear her, watching the girls, who, now that all the excitement was over, had tripped, giggling and chattering, into the cottage garden.

'Eeh . . . like a flock of starlings, aren't they?' Mr Dale said, beaming after them. 'Well, now, Miss Grainger, shall we go inside and look round?'

Laura followed him, but she wasn't going to let him drop the subject of Josh Kern.

'Was it his father who sold this cottage to the present owner?' she asked the estate agent, who looked reluctantly at her, as he unlocked the front door.

'Jack Kern didn't sell it to her, he gave it,' he said at last, rolling an expressive eye, and Laura's brows shot up.

'Gave it?'

'Oh, aye,' he said, waving her past him into the cottage. The models surged in after her and spread out around the ground floor of the cottage like spilt marbles, running from room to room, shouting to each other.

Mr Dale gestured around them. 'The current owner had this porch hallway built on to the front of the cottage. The front door used to open right on to the parlour—that was how they built them a couple of hundred years ago. Through here, miss. There were two little rooms downstairs which have been knocked into one big one.'

Laura walked into the sunlit room and looked with pleasure at the rough stone walls, the arched fireplace with a blue slate hearth, the polished floorboards on which lay a few scattered blue and white rugs. There was a minimum of furniture— dark blue velvet curtains, a couch upholstered in matching material, piled with white and blue cushions, an armchair by the fire, covered in the same velvet, a writing desk, and a couple of book- cases on either side of the fire.

'It's a bit stark, to my taste,' Mr Dale apologised.

Laura gave him a quick look and didn't tell him that it was exactly to her own taste. 'Has it always been like this? Or did the present owner...what did you say her name was?'

'Forest,' he said. 'Mrs Joanna Forest. Yes, she tells me she had the cottage modernised when she moved in twenty years ago. It had been a bit of a mess—it was a farm cottage since it was built, used by the head cowman. No money had ever been spent on it before. First thing she did was strip off all the old wallpaper, and then the plaster, laid the actual stone walls bare, the way they are now. Did it all herself, she said. Quite a job for a woman.' His face was wryly knowing. 'But then she didn't have anything much else to do.'

'She didn't have a job?' Laura was fascinated. She felt she would like Mrs Forest, judging by her taste. She wondered how old the woman was, and what she looked like? Why had she decided to sell the cottage?

'Depends what you mean by a job,' Mr Dale said, winking at her. 'She was...let's say...a friend...of old Jack Kern, Josh's father, who died a year ago.'

'Oh,' Laura said, eyes widening. 'Oh, I see.' So that was why Josh Kern didn't like her?

Lowering his voice, Mr Dale said, 'Aye, I'm not one to gossip, but it's common talk around here—you'd hear the tale in any pub for miles. Everyone knew what was going on. He visited her here every evening, they say. Never slept up at the farmhouse, if you get my meaning. What his wife thought of that, nobody ever found out. Nell Kern's the grim and silent type...'

'His wife was still living with him?'

'Oh, aye. Nell's still there now, running the house for Josh. There's just the two of them living there now. A wonderful housekeeper, Nell—people swear by her cooking, too—but that marriage never worked. Not that she's bad-looking. Even now she's what I'd call a handsome woman. In fact, when we were young, Nell Bevan could have taken her pick of men around here. I didn't have the brass to make her an offer, but I had my eye on her, I tell you! Jack Kern was thought a very lucky man to get her. What went wrong nobody's sure, but... well, who knows what goes on inside a marriage? They just weren't happy together, it seems.'

The other girls surged into the room. 'Oh, the kitchen's lovely, Laura—come and see!' They caught her hands and pulled her after them.

'My wife was taken by it too when she came round with me,' said Mr Dale, following. 'She likes to have a peer at places I'm selling. Very interested in houses is my Doris. And the kitchen was her favourite room in this house.'

Laura loved it, too. Like the sitting-room it had been stripped back to the stone walls, and the fittings were all of golden, polished pine which shone in the sunlight. It was surprisingly spacious and was obviously intended for use as a dining-room, too, judging by the large pine table and chairs set out by a long window at one end.

But even while she looked around, smiling, part of her mind was busy with what Mr Dale had told her about the family background, which explained Josh Kern's hostility. No wonder he had resented his father's gift of this cottage to the woman who had usurped his mother's place.

'Now upstairs,' said the girls and stampeded off with Laura and Mr Dale in the rear.

'I suppose there's no doubt that the cottage does belong to this Mrs Forest?' Laura asked him and he shook his head.

'No, don't you worry about that...you won't have any legal problems.'

Laura gave him an uncertain look. 'You're sure about that?'

'Certain. Don't worry. Josh was just trying to scare you off; take no notice of his threats. He can't legally deny you access to this place, and he knows it. I promise you, Mrs Forest's title has been tested in court; there are no problems.'

He might be telling her the strict truth, but Laura still had doubts about the wisdom of going ahead with buying the cottage.

He saw her expression and grimaced. 'Look, frankly, miss, it did look as if there might be a problem with it because when he gave the cottage to her old Jack Kern didn't do it through his lawyer, daft old beezer. I suppose he didn't want any talk. Not that he had a chance in hell of stopping talk! Not around here. Breath of life to them, a juicy scandal. Anyway, Jack just wrote her a letter—very private letter, too, a love letter—saying he was giving her this cottage so that she could either live here, or sell the cottage, to provide for her future.'

Laura frowned. 'Just a letter? But surely that isn't a legally binding document?'

'Aye, it was, the way he phrased it. It was like a codicil to his will, you see. The lawyer had that, but Jack's letter was dated later than the will, so it was a legal codicil, and Jack had left a sealed letter with his lawyer which said the same thing. Well, when Jack died, Josh Kern challenged her right to the place. She stayed on here until the court found in her favour, because she was afraid that, if she left, Josh Kern would take possession and she would never get it back. The court decided in her favour, and then she moved out and asked me to sell the place for her.'

'She moved away out of the area?' asked Laura, walking into the main bedroom at the front of the cottage.

'She's living in Salisbury with a widowed sister.' Mr Dale looked around with more approval. 'Now this is my favourite room—very pretty.'

Laura looked at the cream wallpaper sprigged with pink, the curtains in pale pink wool, the frilled pink lampshades on the small bedside tables on each side of the double bed, which had a cream coverlet.

The deep-piled carpet was cream, too. It was a very soothing, ultra-feminine room.

'When will she move her furniture out?' asked Laura, as Mr Dale showed her the en suite bathroom leading out of the bedroom.

'She's taken what she wanted, all her personal things—letters, photographs, ornaments. But she didn't want the furniture. I'm to sell it in auction, unless whoever buys the cottage wants it. I got the feeling she wanted to shut the door on it all, forget her years here.'

Suddenly Laura was moved, her green eyes filling with sympathy. 'She may regret that later.'

'She may, that's what I told her,' he said in his gruff voice, his weathered face blank. 'But she didn't change her mind.'

Laura looked around her, sighing. 'Well, if I do eventually buy it, I'd like the furniture—and I'd always let her have it back if she did change her mind later. It seems terribly sad to turn her back on twenty years of her life!'

'That's very kind of you, miss. So, what do you think, then? Going to buy it?'

'I like it, Mr Dale,' Laura cautiously said, 'but you'll appreciate that my fiancé must see it before we make a decision. As soon as he is well enough we'll come back to look at it again. I'll ring you within the week, I expect.'

He nodded, not surprised. 'Aye, well, remember I'll be showing other clients around it in the meantime, and it is a bargain, especially fully furnished. Don't wait too long, Miss Grainger.'

She nodded. 'I'll be in touch as soon as my fiancé is better.' Then she had called the models, who had come trooping out from other rooms.

'Back in the car, girls; we'll have to hurry to get back to York in time for your second session!'

'Bye bye, Mr Dale,' the girls chirped, waving scarlet-tipped fingers at him, and he had grinned back at them appreciatively.

'Nice to meet you, girls.' Then he shook Laura's hand in his bone-scrunching way, nodding at her. 'I'll hope to hear from you soon, then, Miss Grainger, and don't you fret about Josh Kern. His bark is worse than his bite.'

She hoped so. His bark was quite bad enough. A thought occurred to her and she asked, 'By the way, did he say he had offered to buy the cottage?'

'No, he made an offer, and she refused it.'

'Why? Was it too low?'

'No, he offered a good enough price.' Mr Dale paused, frowning. 'I forgot to tell you, with all the harassment we got from Josh...there is a covenant on the cottage, to the effect that whoever buys it must not resell to Josh Kern while Mrs Forest is alive.'

Startled, Laura stared. 'That can't be legally binding, surely?'

'If you don't sign the covenant, she won't sell, and if you do sign the covenant it's legally binding,' said Mr Dale with one of his shrewd grimaces.

Laura had forgotten to tell Patrick about that. She must remember to tell him tomorrow when she rang. It might make a difference to his decision;

such a binding agreement might be a problem later if they wanted to sell and couldn't find a buyer.

They might then wish they could sell to Josh Kern, although Laura was already feeling very sympathetic towards Mrs Forest's desire to keep him out of the property. It would give her a lot of pleasure to do anything that annoyed Josh Kern.

She only hoped she wouldn't see much of him, if she and Patrick did decide to buy Fern Cottage. She bit her lower lip. Why pretend she wasn't sure? She wanted the place. She had loved it on sight, and when she'd seen the beautifully restored interior she had wanted it badly. If someone else bought it before Patrick could see it she was going to be very disappointed.

In fact, it was exactly a week before she and Patrick drove out along the Castle Howard road again, and Mr Dale had been too busy, he said, to come with them, so he had given them the key to the cottage and left them to view the place alone.

'Lucky he was busy. I much prefer to view a house without having an agent hovering about trying to push us into a quick decision,' Patrick said cheerfully as they turned on to the rough track which led to the cottage.

Laura was driving, but her concentration wasn't quite as fixed as usual. She kept looking across the fields on either side, her body tense, half expecting Josh Kern to appear at any moment. She had a shrewd idea why Mr Dale had been too busy to come out here again. She felt the same: she would rather not face Josh Kern again, even with Patrick there. In fact, having Patrick there somehow made it more nerve-racking, because Josh Kern didn't look as if he would use violence against a woman. His face had been contemptuous and hostile, but she hadn't actually been afraid of him. But Patrick was a man, and she sensed that Josh Kern's rules would be very different with another man.

He might well push Patrick into a fight, and, much as she loved him, Laura knew Patrick was no fighter and never had been; he wasn't a coward, he just lacked aggression. He believed in negotiation, not confrontation, discussion, not argument. Patrick was a reconstructed man, wanting to live peacefully in the world, in harmony with his friends and his woman.

Laura's mouth curled in a little smile as she looked sideways at him, and Patrick caught that glance and asked, 'What? What are you smiling at? Tell me the joke.'

'I was just thinking how much I love you,' she said, leaning over to kiss him.

Just as their mouths touched, a horse leapt over a hedge right next to the car.

Laura gave a sharp cry, instinctively ducking her head. Patrick went white. Out of the corner of her eye, Laura saw the big black animal leap over the bonnet, tucking its hooves neatly under it as it sailed across in front of the windscreen. She had to admire the precision of the jump and the way the horse swung round on landing and galloped on down the lane before slowing, turning, and coming back towards the car at a slow trot.

'Is that . . . ?' Patrick whispered in a dazed voice.

'Yes,' Laura grimly said. 'That's him. Josh Kern.'

'He must be out of his mind!' Patrick's hands were not quite steady and he still looked pale.

'Way out,' she agreed, scrambling out of the car as the black horse came to a halt next to it. Laura stared angrily up at the rider, her green eyes glittering with the resentment of someone who had just had a physical shock.

'You madman!' she yelled at him. 'What a crazy, dangerous thing to do!'

'How was I to know your car was parked there?' Josh Kern drawled, smiling with mockery in a way that told her he had known very well that their car was there before he jumped, and that, what was more, he'd recognised it from her last visit. 'When I'm riding over my own land I don't expect to find trespassers hiding behind every hedge,' he added smoothly.

Very flushed, Laura snapped, 'I'd have thought that, even if you didn't care whether or not you killed us, you'd have minded killing your horse. Or don't you think animals matter?'

His smile went. 'If I'd thought for an instant that my horse might get hurt I wouldn't have taken that jump!' he bit out, and she believed him.

The black horse tossed its head as if in agreement with its master, shifting its feet, the hooves scraping on flint in the track, and Laura was glad there was a car between them. The horse, like the man, was a big brute.

Laura looked from the horse to its master, whose beige-jodhpur-clad thighs effortlessly controlled the animal without needing to use the reins which lay loosely in his tanned hands. Open-necked shirt, dark tweed hacking jacket, a black riding hat on his black hair, polished black leather boots knee-high, Josh Kern belonged against this background—the rolling fields, the stone walls, and elms just coming into leaf. Laura had a sinking feeling in the pit of her stomach, and couldn't account for it. Or was it just that he looked so much at home here, and she and Patrick didn't?

Aware of her scrutiny, Josh Kern's sardonic grey eyes wandered over her coolly, from her blonde head to her small, delicately shod feet.

She and Patrick were going to a wedding after lunch, that afternoon, and Laura was elegantly dressed in a cream silk suit with gold buttons—an outfit from a young British designer, in classical style, the skirt straight-fitting, with a little pleat at the back, the jacket tight-waisted, with long sleeves. In honour of the occasion, she had tied her blonde hair on top of her head in a gold bow, letting it fall in a shower of ringlets around her face.

From Josh Kern's expression he wasn't impressed. No doubt he, too, was thinking that she was from the city, she didn't belong around here. She saw his mouth twist, then he lifted his stare to meet her eyes.

'You're the model who came last week,' he said, pretending surprise, although she was certain he had recognised her car and that was why he had jumped his black horse right over the bonnet.

'I'm not a model! I don't know where you got that idea,' she told him sharply.

He shrugged. 'Something Dale said, I think. Yes, he said you were all models.'

'The girls with me were all models; I'm not one!'

'No?' His eyes went wandering again. 'You look like a model to me.'

She knew it wasn't intended as flattery. Josh Kern had made his views on models very plain when she was here before. All the same, under his assessment, a little flush crept up her face, especially when his gaze lingered on her long, slender legs.

'Very chic,' he drawled, and she felt Patrick stiffen next to her, resenting the personal nature of the remark.

Josh Kern hadn't so much as acknowledged Patrick's presence yet, even by looking in his direction. No doubt, Laura thought, he found her an easier target, an idea which made her bristle from head to foot like a cat that is having its fur stroked the wrong way.

'So what do you do if you aren't a model?'

'I'm in public relations,' she curtly told him, and he raised his brows in sardonic enquiry.

'I've often wondered what that meant—are you some sort of journalist?'

'No,' she said coolly, aware that he was making fun of her, but taking his question totally seriously. 'My firm is a buffer between a client company and the public, or the media. I deal with the Press, TV, radio, on behalf of the company, or arrange for publicity for them—when they're launching a new product, for instance—smooth their way, make their lives easier, entertain overseas buyers for them.'

'Ah, I see,' he murmured, his mouth twisting cynically. 'So that was why you had a carload of

model girls with you? Were you all going off to
"entertain" some overseas buyers the other day? I
hope you gave them a good time.'

The insult made her flush hotly, and Patrick lost
his temper. 'Now look here, Mr Kern,' he burst out,
'that's enough! You're being damned rude...'

Josh Kern turned his dark head, and stared at
him with icily arrogant indifference.

'And who the hell are you?' He took in Patrick's
appearance with a dismissive flick of the eyes,
noting that he was dressed as formally and elegantly as Laura, in a smooth pale grey suit, ex-
pensively tailored, a crisp white shirt and a dove-
grey silk tie, his black shoes shining like mirrors.

'I'm Patrick Ogilvie, Laura's fiancé! And I resent
your tone, Mr Kern!'

Josh Kern flicked a look at Laura. 'You're going
to marry *him*?'

'Yes,' she snapped, tense as she waited for what
he might say next.

What he did was laugh. In a way that made her
burn with rage. He looked Patrick up and down
again, his black brows signalling contempt and
amusement.

'Now, he has *got* to be a model!'

Patrick went red.

'I'm an artist, as it happens!' If he had ever
thought she was exaggerating her description of
Josh Kern, Laura thought, he certainly wouldn't
after this! The man was living up to everything she
had said about him.

'An artist? Not a model?' Those black brows shot
up, signalling disbelief. 'You amaze me. But I bet

you work for glossy magazines, or do the artwork for an advertising firm.'

'I'm freelance; I do whatever I'm commissioned to do, Mr Kern,' Patrick said with dignity, refusing to apologise for his work or himself, and, proud of him, Laura moved to his side and slipped her hand through his arm, leaning on him. Patrick glanced down at her and then looked back at Josh Kern, his face smoothing out into courtesy again.

'I'm sorry you dislike the idea of having us living in the cottage, Mr Kern. I realise the circumstances are difficult for you, but be fair—it's hardly our fault that the owner doesn't wish to sell it back to you.'

Josh Kern's face tightened and darkened, but he didn't say anything when Patrick paused to let him.

After a moment, Patrick went on quietly, 'Somebody is going to buy the place, you know. Sooner or later. You might as well accept the idea.'

Josh Kern's teeth parted and he bit out, 'Like hell. I can't stop you buying this place...' His narrowed stare shot from Patrick to Laura, glittering and dangerous. 'But, believe me, you aren't going to enjoy living here!'

Laura's head went back, her blonde curls blowing in the spring wind, her eyes defiant. 'If you keep threatening us, you'll find yourself in trouble with the police, Mr Kern!'

'Threatening you? I wasn't threatening you,' he lied blandly. 'I was warning you. About the inconvenience you're going to suffer when I put my grids across the track.'

'Grids?' she repeated, thrown by that word. 'What do you mean, grids?'

'Cattle grids,' he coolly said. 'I have a very valuable herd of cows and I don't want them straying off my land, so I'm having gates put up at the end of our *private* road and there will be a wide cattle grid in front. I should have done it before, but we're so far off the beaten track that I hadn't thought it was necessary, but now I think I will have to get it done without delay.'

'That won't inconvenience us,' Laura told him. 'I've often driven over cattle grids; my car can cope with them, and so can Patrick's. As for the gates, you'll still have to allow us free access. It will be very expensive for both sides if you make me prove my rights in court, but I will, believe me, if I have to!'

He didn't argue with that, just murmured, 'It will take weeks to do the work on the road, by the way. Sorry about that; there will be quite a mess.'

She laughed scornfully. 'What? A set of gates and a cattle grid? I wouldn't have thought so. Unless you deliberately drag it out, just to make life difficult!'

His hard mouth mocked her. 'Well, you know country workmen—they never hurry themselves. Amazing how long they can take to do one simple little job. And the ground is pretty rocky there; they'll probably have to use pneumatic drills, I expect, which will be noisy for you, especially as they start very early in the morning. Crack of dawn, probably.'

'I won't need an alarm clock, then, will I?' she threw back, her face angrily flushed.

His grey eyes gleamed. 'And the road will be covered with mud, I'm afraid, especially if it rains, of course, and with the cows going backwards and forwards along this road morning and night, from their field to the milking shed and back again, twice a day, it does get very messy.'

'No doubt you'll have done the work before we move in!'

'When are you moving in?' he softly asked, but Laura didn't answer. He obviously meant to tell the workmen to start digging the very week she told him she was moving into the cottage.

She wasn't telling Josh Kern anything. He made the hair stand up on the back of her neck just by looking at her.

CHAPTER THREE

PATRICK loved the cottage, just as Laura had known he would. It was so exactly what they had been looking for, and the price was well within their means. All the same, he hesitated over buying it.

'Josh Kern is going to make a very unpleasant neighbour, Laura. Who needs that? We're buying somewhere in the country because we want a peaceful life, have you forgotten?'

'No, of course I haven't,' she claimed, although increasingly she kept forgetting why she was thinking of buying a country home, and only knew that nothing would make her back down in front of Josh Kern. She looked up at Patrick stubbornly. 'But I'm not going to let that great brute bully us into going away!'

'Well, I don't believe in giving in to bullies, either, Laura, you know that. Don't think I didn't resent the way he talked to you; it made me furious!'

'I resented it, too, and he was just as offensive to you!' Her green eyes were fever-bright, and Patrick gave her a startled look.

'Darling, he really did put you in a temper, didn't he? I've never seen you like this!'

Laura had never felt like this before. 'I'm not letting him drive me away, Patrick!' she insisted.

'But, Laura ... do you really think this cottage is worth so much aggro?'

'Yes!' she stubbornly said. Her mind was in turmoil, a confusion of contradictory emotions she didn't understand battling inside her, but one thing she was certain about. Josh Kern had challenged her to this fight, and all her female instincts made her determined not to give in to him.

Patrick loved her and was reluctant to deny her anything she had set her heart on, but he was a man who liked to live in harmony with his surroundings, so he was difficult to persuade. Only when he saw she wouldn't change her mind did he give in at last. 'I only hope we aren't making a serious mistake,' he said, though, with a troubled expression.

'Don't worry,' Laura said, 'I think Josh Kern's threats are just blustering. He may try to make a nuisance of himself at first, but if we ignore him he'll soon get bored with that!'

'As long as he doesn't keep driving his cows backwards and forwards outside the cottage!' groaned Patrick. 'Can you imagine what that track would look like after a few days of that? Especially if he has workmen digging holes all over the place!'

Laura laughed. 'Oh, poor Patrick, are you going to hate it? Well, we can always buy a big dog and have it barking at his cows to drive them away.'

'I hate dogs, especially big ones!' he said, making her laugh even more.

Mr Dale, however, was delighted to have made a sale. 'I had a feeling you would buy it; I nearly always sense when someone's serious about a property! And you'll be getting a bargain with this one. There's not much work to be done, except on the roof. A few slates blew off in the last spring gale; we've had them replaced, but I expect you'll need to do a little more work on that roof—it is quite an old place. And as you'll have noticed, some rain got in upstairs, but that's nothing serious. You'll probably want to redecorate, but it isn't necessary. No, you're getting a real bargain.'

'What about this farmer?' Patrick asked, and Mr Dale laughed merrily.

'Oh, Josh Kern's bark is worse than his bite,' he said, as he had said to Laura.

Patrick did not look convinced. 'Don't talk about barking,' he said, baffling the estate agent.

Laura explained, and Mr Dale grinned at them. 'Good idea; cows will always run away from a barking dog—but be careful Josh Kern doesn't shoot it. He'd be entitled, if it chased his stock.'

'He wouldn't?' Laura asked, aghast, then met Mr Dale's wry eyes and winced. 'He would,' she agreed slowly. 'No dog, Patrick.'

He looked relieved.

On the following Monday, Laura contacted her solicitor to ask him to act for her, and then, with a sigh of relief at being able to forget about Josh Kern, she turned her attention to work.

The firm had a number of local clients, but the most important was Eyre-York, a textile company with offices in York and a large mill in North Yorkshire, which exported its man-made textiles all over the world. To attract clients from overseas, the managing director and chief shareholder, Ian Eyre, liked to have special events, flamboyant occasions, which Laura's firm organised for him. Over the past two years they had given fashion shows in stately homes, on a pleasure boat sailing along the East Yorkshire coast from Scarborough to Whitby, even a Hallowe'en show up at Whitby Abbey, above the little seaside town where Dracula was supposed to have landed. Laura had actually had an actor playing Dracula in evening dress and scarlet-lined black cape moving among the models in their designer dresses. That had been a very successful evening; a lot of orders had come from that.

'We want something as different as that again, Laura,' Ian had told her over lunch the previous week, and that Monday he rang her to see if she had come up with any ideas yet.

'I thought maybe...a fair...' she tentatively suggested. 'With a merry-go-round and dodgem cars and a ghost train—all the usual fairground rides...'

'A fair?' A note of distaste entered Ian Eyre's voice. 'Not quite the image we're trying to promote, is it, Laura?'

He could be acid, although he always tried to give the impression he was totally charming, both to potential buyers of his product, and to any women he met.

A man just hitting forty, he tried to stave off middle age by every means in his power, his lean body carefully preserved with unremitting dieting and relentless exercise. He had been married, but his wife had divorced him some years ago, and so far Ian hadn't been tempted to repeat the experience. He had plenty of women in his life without needing marriage, Laura thought wryly. Patrick called him a smoothie—and the word fitted him exactly. Tall, with sleekly brushed fair hair which so far only had the odd silvery hair showing here and there, he had eyes of a cold pale blue, and he always wore beautifully tailored suits made from his own products and never missed an opportunity to draw attention to their quality, especially with customers from overseas.

His dismissal of her first idea didn't worry her. She had others up her sleeve.

'Well, if you want a classier image... how about a medieval fair? Wool merchants used to take their products to fairs at one time, to sell them, and we could have people in costume manning stalls and fairground rides...swings, coconut shies; we could even get someone to put on a bearskin and pretend to be a dancing bear on a chain...'

'Medieval fair,' Ian thought aloud, his voice interested. 'Hmm...there might be something in that. Get us some sketches and notes and we'll have lunch and discuss it further. How soon can you get that ready?'

'Next week?'

'I'll be in Japan,' he dismissed. 'I get back on the... wait a minute, let my check my diary... yes, the first day of next month. How about lunch the following Wednesday?'

Laura consulted her own diary. 'The fourth? Yes, I'm free then. In the meantime, I'll get Patrick on to sketching out some ideas and I'll have copy typed up for you to read with them. Enjoy Japan and make a lot of sales.'

That was a hectic week for Laura. She had several other projects in hand, and kept juggling them all, rushing here and there and talking endlessly so that she was exhausted every night when she went home, and didn't have the energy to see Patrick. She wasn't even there the day he brought a portfolio of sketches of medieval fairs in to the office, and had to ring him to tell him how much she had liked them.

'They were terrific, exactly what I wanted!' she said with enthusiasm, the sketches spread out on her desk, her eyes roaming over the images they suggested . . . gaily coloured stalls around which milled people in medieval costume, merchants displaying their clothes to men carrying pomanders against the smell of the crowds, peasants with children buying gingerbread from one stall or watching the jugglers and conjurors, fire-eaters, men on stilts and even a dancing bear on a chain.

'And it will be easy to come up with the circus performers, although it will cost your client quite a bit,' Patrick said.

'He won't mind that. He'll love it,' she said. 'When he sees your sketches, I'm sure Ian will go for the medieval fair theme. It's colourful and different and will give his foreign buyers a day out. Patrick, you're wonderful.'

'I think you are too,' he said, laughing. 'It was all your idea; I just came up with what you asked for. How about lunch today?'

'Sorry, darling,' she said absently, 'I'm lunching a client.'

'Dinner?'

She sighed. 'I'm booked, Patrick—that bald guy from Hospers; we're taking a crowd of foreign buyers to dinner. I'm sorry, I just don't have time for a private life at the moment,' she said distractedly, one eye on the clock. 'But this rush will be over by the end of next week, I hope.'

'I need to talk to you now, Laura—not next week!'

She picked up the irritated note in his voice and frowned, surprised. Patrick was never irritable. 'Is something wrong?'

'Not wrong, exactly,' he said, sounding less impatient. 'The fact is...Laura, I've been asked to illustrate a series of children's books—international fairy stories and legends, by Rae Dunhill.'

'Rae Dunhill?' Laura knew the name, although she had never read any of the author's books, which were all for children. 'Oh, that's quite an accolade, Patrick! She's supposed to be very good.'

'I've read a couple, and she's better than that,' he told her with feeling. 'She's amazing. And she's becoming a really big best seller, apparently. I certainly think she's the best living children's writer...and, Laura...she asked for me, personally, to illustrate her books!' Excitement crept into his voice and Laura began to smile, her eyes affectionate.

'She's got good taste, then! She may be the best children's writer—but you're definitely the best illustrator around today.'

He laughed, not displeased but a little wry. 'Well, thanks, but then you would say that, wouldn't you? You're prejudiced! But that wasn't what I wanted to tell you, or rather that wasn't all. You see ... Laura, she ... Rae Dunhill, I mean ... and the publisher, too, the editor, anyway ... they want me to go abroad ...'

'Abroad?' she interrupted, startled.

'Yes, to the places in the stories she's writing, to get the right look for my illustrations. She wants background pictures, you see.... She thought of line-drawings behind the text on some pages, and full-colour pages of places, like Venice, or Paris; a medieval look for some stories, Celtic or Viking for others! And to get it right, I'll have to go to the art galleries, see paintings of the period, and costume museums ...' His voice trailed away, and then he said, 'It would mean being away for weeks, though.'

'But why can't you use reference books for that? You usually do.'

'That's just the point. Rae says everyone uses the same books, takes their ideas from the same artists and pictures—there's no freshness any more. The artwork in this new series is going to be as important as the text, and Rae wants something new and different and ...' He broke off, laughed a little shakily. 'Well, inspired!'

'A trip like that will cost a lot of money—are the publishers paying for it?'

'All my expenses!' he said, then added more cautiously, 'Well, within reason, anyway. Just think of it, Laura—Italy, France, Germany, Holland, Denmark! I'll fly, of course, and I'll spend at least a week in each one. Of course I've been to Italy three or four times, and Holland and France, too, but I've never been to Germany or Denmark, and it's ages since I was abroad, anyway; isn't it wonderful?'

'No wonder you're excited! It will be the trip of a lifetime!' Out of the corner of her eye Laura saw her secretary looking pointedly at her watch. Laura bit her lip. 'Patrick, sorry, but I've got to go; I'm meeting a client for lunch... Darling, I'm absolutely thrilled for you, and I can't wait to hear all the details about your trip. How about dinner next Friday?'

He sighed. 'Oh, well. OK, darling. Shall I do your usual weekend shopping today? It's no trouble; I shall be doing mine, anyway. I'll take it over to your flat and put it away, shall I? And while I'm there I might as well check that the flat is tidy; if you're so busy I suppose you haven't had time to do any housework this week.'

'You're an angel, Patrick!' In fact, Laura's flat was almost immaculate—she had hardly been home over the past week except to go to bed exhausted and sleep like the dead. But it was typical of Patrick to be so thoughtful and she blew him a kiss down the phone. 'Love you.'

As she put the phone down she surprised a look on her secretary's face which puzzled her at the time, but later that afternoon, in a taxi on her way back to the office, she suddenly realised what she had seen in Anne's dark eyes. Disapproval. Now why on earth should Anne disapprove of her blowing a kiss to her fiancé? Laura knew that her secretary could be rather shy—almost prim—but she hadn't had her down as that sort of prude.

Or had Anne disapproved of the idea of Patrick doing the housework for her? Laura's mouth curled in wry amusement. Now that she could believe. Anne was very conventional and traditional in everything, including how she expected men to act. And women, come to that!

By the time Ian Eyre got back from Japan life had quietened down considerably for Laura, and she had heard all about Patrick's forthcoming trip to Europe, and ruefully expressed her envy.

'I wish I was going!'

'Come with me,' he promptly said, and she was tempted, but sighed.

'I'd love to, but it's impossible. I just have too much work on hand at present.'

'You could delegate!'

She gave him a dry look. 'Who to? There's nobody in the firm I could trust to do my work.'

'Nobody's indispensable, Laura! And I'll be away for six or seven weeks, remember!'

'I know, and I'll miss you,' she said, kissing him. 'But I can't just drop what I'm doing and fly off to Europe with you, Patrick. I only wish I could. When do you go?'

'In a fortnight.'

He was looking sulky and she slid her arms around his neck, indulgent regret in her green eyes. 'Don't look like that!' His lips had turned down, his face grown reproachful; he looked like a cross little boy.

'Surely you can manage some time off in the next month or so?'

Laura thought, sighing. 'Well, I might be able to get a weekend off while you're in Paris, maybe even another one when you're in Holland. I could fly over on a Friday and get back late on Sunday evening.'

He looked down into her eyes. 'Will you do that, then?'

She nodded, and his face broke into smiles once more. Laura laughed up at him. 'I see. Feeling better now, are we, now that we've got our own way?'

'I feel lost when you're not there, Laura; I need you,' he said in that little-boy voice, and she hugged him, very touched.

'I'll always be there for you, Patrick.' Yet, not for the first time, she had a faint quiver of uneasiness, although she couldn't quite put her finger on what disturbed her. It was just that...oh, although Patrick did so much for her, and she loved him so much, she knew, deep down, that he needed her more than she needed him, and that somehow worried her, although she didn't know why it should.

When she met Ian Eyre for lunch he was enthusiastic about the medieval fair theme for his buyers' day, and took away with him the portfolio containing Patrick's sketches and her plans for the way the fair would be used to display Eyre-York materials.

'I've already spoken to my head designer about the idea and he has come up with some marvellous designs for clothes that would echo the theme— long, scalloped sleeves on dresses, for instance. That sort of thing. He's quite keen to do it—it gives him something new and exciting to work with. So well done, Laura. Now I must show these sketches to my board and I'll give you the final go-ahead once they've agreed on the scheme. Then you can go ahead and work out the final details for the fair itself—you can get hold of the fair people, I presume?' He gestured to the sketches. 'Jugglers and fire-eaters et cetera?'

She nodded. 'Yes, of course.' Patrick had helped considerably in that direction, too, because some time in the past he had worked with a travelling fair, sketching and painting them for a book. Patrick had got in touch with them again this week, and the manager had agreed to co-operate, although the sum he required for his services had made Laura groan.

'Which brings us to the big question—cost,' said Ian, eyeing her drily and perhaps reading her expression correctly. 'How much, Laura? What will it all cost?'

She smiled brightly, took a deep breath and told him.

Ian whistled. 'That's a joke, right?'

She shook her head and handed him another folder containing several sheets of paper detailing costs. 'As you'll see in this breakdown of the figures, most of it is the fee demanded by the fair people, Ian. After all, they won't be earning, because your buyers won't be paying for their rides, and so on. So they want a firm figure up front if they're to co-operate.'

'Daylight robbery,' Ian said. 'Did you get quotes from other fairs?'

Laura gave him a wry look. 'No, but I can, if you insist—it will delay everything, of course.'

'Hmm...' he said, his face sardonic. 'I see. Well, I'll put it up to my board, anyway, and let you know.'

The day Patrick was due to leave for Europe Ian rang her to say that his board of directors had accepted her plan.

'The cost made them blink, but these events usually pay off in the end. Try to keep costs down as much as possible, though, Laura. Go ahead and make all the final arrangements your end, and I'll see that our designs are ready for the big day. Keep in touch.'

Laura was able to tell Patrick this good news when she saw him off from Heathrow, on the first leg of his journey, promising to meet him in Paris the following weekend.

'I'm convinced it was your sketches that won Ian's board over, darling. You will be back in time for the fair, won't you? It will be terrific fun.'

'I should be,' he agreed uncertainly. 'It all depends on Rae Dunhill. If the work I'm doing is what she wants I should be home early, but if she isn't satisfied I might have to retrace my steps and do the work again.'

'Tell her to get knotted,' Laura said indignantly, and he laughed.

'If you knew her, you'd realise I couldn't do that. She's terrifying, knows exactly what she wants, and is determined to get it.'

His flight for Copenhagen was called and he had to go, kissing Laura hurriedly before he fled. 'See you in Paris!'

During the following week Laura was busy until the Thursday afternoon when she found herself with very little to do, so she decided to take the rest of the day off and drive out to the cottage to take measurements for new curtains which Patrick had decided to make for some of the rooms.

She got the key from Mr Dale and an hour later was standing on a ladder measuring the windows in a back bedroom when she heard a sound downstairs.

Laura froze, listening intently. Had she imagined the faint creak, as if someone was creeping about in one of the rooms? It was easy to imagine things in an empty house, especially if you were alone. An old house like this must be full of little creaks and murmurs.

A moment later she knew it wasn't her imagination. Someone began to come up the stairs. The tread was heavy, loud. That wasn't a woman, thought Laura, her skin cold. No woman walked that heavily. That was a man. How had he got in? She was sure she had closed the front door behind her. It wasn't in her nature to be careless over closing doors.

She came down the step-ladder as quietly as she could and looked around for a weapon. The best she could come up with was a chair. She got behind the door with it raised over her head, ready to smash it down on anyone who came into the room, if he seemed dangerous. From where she stood she would be able to see the man clearly in the dressing-table mirror as soon as he walked into the room.

She could hear the intruder moving on the landing; the floorboards were old and gave protestingly under every footfall.

Laura concentrated on every tiny sound, guessing what the intruder was doing. She heard doors being opened and closed again almost at once, so that she knew he wasn't searching each room, just looking in and immediately shutting the door. What was he looking for? Valuable objects?

Or...her? Her mouth went dry. Had someone seen her arrive, realised she was in here, alone?

If he had, and had come in after her, then... She felt cold sweat trickle down her back at the thought of what would be on his mind.

Only then did she realise how isolated the cottage was, how far away from any other human habitation. If she screamed nobody would hear her. Why hadn't it dawned on her before?

The footsteps approached the door behind which she stood. Laura barely breathed, fixed and waiting. The handle turned. The door began to open. Laura tightened her grip on the chair, staring at the mirror, her body tensed.

A man's shape swam into view in the mirror. For a second she simply registered the masculinity. A powerful man: broad shoulders, deep chest. Disturbing. His clothes were working clothes—a green and white check shirt, open at the throat, his sleeves rolled up to the elbow showing strong brown forearms; he wore olive-green cord trousers, held at the waist by a wide black leather belt.

She saw all that in a hurried glance, then focused on his face, poised to smash the chair down on his head when he took one last step into the room, bringing him close enough.

But she didn't. Because she recognised that face, and realised he was watching her, too, in the mirror. His reflected eyes gave her a sardonic stare.

All the breath seemed to leave her body in one long gasp. Relief? Surprise? Or something else? She didn't know.

'What the hell are you doing standing up there with that chair?' Josh Kern drawled, and Laura shakily lowered it, reddening and feeling silly as she put the chair down.

'I thought you were a burglar!'

His black brows lifted. 'Well, I'm glad you waited before you brought that thing down on my head; it would have given me a very nasty headache.'

'You're lucky I waited to make sure you were a burglar before I hit you,' Laura told him.

'I'm glad you did!' he drawled.

It wasn't easy getting down from the chair while those cool grey eyes watched her. Laura tried to do it with all the dignity she could muster.

It was unfortunate that she was so tense that she missed her footing and stumbled, crashing into the door and knocking over the chair she had just put down.

Josh Kern moved fast. One minute she was lurching towards the floor, and next he had grabbed her around the waist with both hands.

She gasped in shock at his touch, her face suddenly burning. This close to the man, she realised just how much taller and more powerful than her he was—she had never felt particularly small or weak before. At this moment she felt both. She felt tiny and helpless and very vulnerable, especially when she remembered that she was alone in the house with him.

'You should be more careful, working here alone,' Josh Kern softly said, one of his hands sliding round her waist. Like a snake encircling its prey, she thought, shuddering.

Laura tried to step back, away from him, but his arm had become an iron band. She couldn't break his hold on her.

'I'm OK, let me go,' she said shakily.

'Did you hurt yourself?' was all he said in reply, and he made no move to free her.

She shook her head, her blonde hair dishevelled, brushing against his sleeve. This close to him, his scent was in her nostrils—a clean, male fragrance, fresh air, earth, grass.

'Sure? I thought you hit the door...no bruises anywhere?' He ran a slow, exploring hand down her side, brushing the swell of her breast, her waist, her slim hip and down to her thigh, and Laura felt a strange heat growing under her skin everywhere he touched her.

Drawing a shaken, audible breath, she muttered, 'Mr Kern, get your hands off me! Do I have to hit you after all?'

He laughed in his throat, huskily, but let go of her, and Laura hurriedly moved away from him.

'How did you get in here, Mr Kern?' she attacked. 'I closed the front door when I came in—

I know I did. Have you got a key? You shouldn't
have; you don't own the cottage and you have no
right to walk in and out as you please.'

He pushed his hands into the pockets of his well-
worn green cords and shrugged indifferently.

'The front door was open. It's very windy today,
and that latch is rather worn. You should lock the
door, not just close it. Better remember that in
future.'

His tone was bland, but Laura didn't quite believe his explanation; she was sure the latch had
clicked home, or that she would have heard the
wind blow the door open, if that was what had
happened.

Another explanation occurred to her. 'Did your
father have a key to the cottage? Is that it? I suppose
you found it after his death, and have been able to
come and go here just as you liked!'

His face changed. The hard angles of it tightened,
the grey eyes blazing. She took a step backwards
in alarm.

'Don't ever ... ever ... talk about my father, or
his private life, to me or anyone else,' he ground
out between his teeth, glaring.

Laura was startled by his reaction. It told her a
lot about Josh Kern. His father might be dead, but
clearly the past wasn't dead with him, not as far as
his son was concerned. He was still bitter about his
father's involvement with the woman who had lived
in this cottage.

Slowly, Laura said in a voice meant to placate
him, 'I'm sorry if I trod on sensitive ground, but
it was an obvious question to ask, and, anyway,

even if the door was open you should have knocked
or called out. You must have known I was in the
cottage; my car is parked outside.'

There was a pause. His scowl smoothed out. 'I
saw you arrive,' he agreed, giving her a veiled look
through dark lashes. 'I've been working on the dry-
stone walls across the field behind here.' He walked
to the window to look, pointing. 'Over there.'

She joined him and followed his gaze. Across a
rough pasture she saw a barrow filled with rough
stones, a few tools piled up on top of them.

'It's thirsty work; my flask of tea ran out just
after lunch,' Josh Kern drawled. 'So when I saw
you drive up, I decided to take a break from the
job and stroll over here, see if you felt neighbourly
enough to give me a cup of tea.'

It was some sort of olive branch, and Laura could
only accept it, although she was reluctant to do so
because something about the man made her very
wary of him.

'Of course,' she said offhandedly. 'Come downstairs; I'll make some tea now.'

'Thanks.' He didn't move though. 'Stuffy in here,
isn't it? You don't want the house to get damp, you
know. Take my advice—open all the windows, get
some air circulating.' He opened the window and
a brisk April wind blew into the room, tossing her
fine blonde hair into wild disorder. 'Sorry,' Josh
Kern said, brushing back some strands which had
been flung across her face.

It happened again—the touch of his cool
fingers accelerating her heartbeat, making it
hard to breathe.

She was so horrified by her own reactions that she turned hurriedly to walk away, and he turned at the same time. She almost walked right into him, stopped dead, her face an inch away from his shirt. He wasn't wearing a tie, and his collar was open, the two top buttons of the shirt undone too, showing her his weathered skin, a scattering of black hairs across his chest.

A hot pulse began beating in Laura's neck. She had a terrifying impulse to lean forward, to put her mouth against that brown skin, breathe in the scent of his body. She stared at his throat, caught a glimpse of those powerful male shoulders, and her body began to burn.

What is wrong with me? she thought wildly. I must be ill. I've got a fever, I'm delirious, hallucinating. This isn't real. I don't even like the man; why should I want to...? But she couldn't bear to admit, even to herself, what she wanted to do. She only knew that she had never in her life felt anything like this sensual turmoil.

'There was no need to jump like that; you're in no danger from me, Miss Grainger,' Josh Kern drily murmured, watching her flushed and agitated face.

She risked a glance upwards, her green eyes flickering restlessly as they met and moved away from his. She had to pull herself together; she mustn't let him imagine that...that what? she asked herself, biting her inner lip at what she did not want Josh Kern to imagine.

'Although I might be in danger from you,' he softly said, and she heard the teasing amusement in his tone with a little shiver.

What did he mean by that? She didn't dare ask.

He told her anyway. 'I keep getting this disconcerting impulse to kiss you, and that wouldn't be a good idea, would it?'

'No,' she said, a little too wildly.

'You are engaged to someone else,' he agreed, but she felt him staring at her mouth, and to her dismay her lips quivered with nervous awareness of that stare.

A second later Josh Kern bent and covered her mouth with his own in a brief, hard kiss. It was over before she had time to think, let alone respond. One minute his lips were moving against hers, and the next he was several feet away.

'Sorry if you hated it, but it can sometimes be more dangerous not to give in to an impulse,' he drily told her. 'You end up getting obsessed with what you've tried to ignore.'

Laura couldn't get a word out. She was too busy trying to ignore an impulse of her own. She was dying to touch her mouth, to trace the imprint of his lips. She felt as if the kiss had left a mark she would be able to pick up with her fingertips. Even more disturbing was the realisation that she badly wanted him to kiss her again.

CHAPTER FOUR

For days afterwards that moment kept coming into Laura's head; she couldn't forget about it, any more than she could understand it.

She didn't even like Josh Kern. He was the sort of man who made her angry, the sort of man her friends seemed to marry and then spend the rest of their time complaining about. She could just imagine his home life. Some woman would wait on him, doing all the cooking, cleaning and washing and ironing his shirts. No doubt his mother, who Mr Dale said was one of the best cooks in Yorkshire. Estranged from her husband, who had another woman living just across the fields, Mrs Kern must have given all her love and attention to her only child. Josh Kern had the arrogant assurance of someone who had been spoilt from birth. He walked the earth as though he owned it.

She loathed men like that. So why...why...was he having this effect on her? No matter how many times she asked the question she never came up with an answer, or not one she wanted to believe.

The following weekend she went to Paris and she and Patrick had a great time together, seeing the sights and eating at wonderful little bistros in back streets recommended by the porter at the hotel at which they were both staying. It wasn't one of the grand hotels of Paris; it was a comfortable little hotel up a side-street on the Left Bank, not far from St-Sulpice.

They walked everywhere because it was easier and cheaper than getting taxis, and anyway, the fine spring weather made walking a pleasure. They followed the Seine, not bothering to use maps of Paris, just using the river as a compass, walking back and forth across the bridges, or wandering along the exclusive shopping streets around the rue de Rivoli, visiting the Louvre, walking up the Champs-Elysées. Sometimes Patrick sketched while she sat down at a terrace café table, drank coffee, or a glass of wine, and watched the flow of Parisian life.

It was an extremely restful weekend; time seemed to trickle past because she had put behind her all the rush and worry of her working week and was just flowing with the tide of the city.

Yet it seemed no time at all between when she stepped off the plane at Charles de Gaulle airport and when she boarded a plane home on Sunday night.

'See you in Amsterdam,' Patrick said, kissing her before she went through to the departure area. 'Sure you couldn't make it to Rome next weekend?'

'I only wish I could,' she sighed regretfully. 'But I'm meeting Mr Hudson down at the cottage...'

'Who?' frowned Patrick.

'The builder,' she reminded, and Patrick's face cleared.

'Oh, yes, the local man Mr Dale recommended! You didn't say you'd been in touch with him.'

'Didn't I? Yes, I rang him and he's going to look around and give us an estimate for the work we need done.'

'You should get several estimates, Laura, you know that. Ring another couple of builders before you give Hudson the job.'

She nodded. 'Of course, I meant to—but apparently Hudson has done all the building work on the cottage for years, and you must admit the modernisation has been well done.'

Patrick agreed. 'So long as his estimate is reasonable, I'll leave it with you to decide, darling. So I'll see you in Amsterdam in three weeks' time.'

He was going to be spending more time in Italy than he had in France. Laura really wished she could spare the time to go there too, but her work wouldn't allow it.

She had a very limited time in which to put together the plans for the medieval fair. Ian Eyre had fixed a day in high summer and Laura had to find a suitable site. Somewhere within easy reach of his factory, and the local airport, with a good road leading to it, yet with plenty of space on which to put the fair. It had to be easy to control access, or they might get gatecrashers who could disrupt the whole day, yet it had to be an attractive area to impress foreign buyers.

Laura had begun to comb her lists of suitable venues, but for one reason or another had had to strike them off one by one. They were either unavailable or didn't fit her criteria.

It didn't help to have Ian ringing up every other day to ask if she had found the right place yet.

'I'll let you know as soon as I have,' she promised him on Friday afternoon, one eye on the clock because she had a meeting with a new client at three and didn't want to be on the phone to Ian when the other man arrived.

'Well, I've had an idea myself, Laura. How about having it at Ransoms?'

'Ransoms?' she echoed blankly.

'My aunt's place; it's about twelve miles north of York, a big house surrounded by parkland. Plenty of space for the fair, and we could set up a marquee beside the fair where people could eat and drink.'

'A medieval banquet would be a good idea,' she suggested, and he flared into enthusiasm.

'Now that is a brilliant idea! Can you arrange that, too, Laura? It might be a bit of a problem to find people to set it up, I suppose, even for you.'

'Oh, I'm sure I can find a caterer for it; lots of stately homes do medieval banquets now. It's not so much the food that's the problem, it's getting the staff to dress up, finding the right costumes to fit them, and persuading them to wear them while they're serving or cooking. Medieval dress has long hanging sleeves that get in the way! But I'll find someone to do it. The food is easy by comparison—roast beef always goes down well at these things, or venison, or maybe a roast goose with an apple in its beak! Pheasant dressed with its feathers after being cooked ... that sort of thing.'

'You've done your homework, haven't you? Or have you done a medieval banquet before?'

She laughed. 'I confess I have, for a cosmetics firm, a couple of years ago. It was a big hit with their American buyers.'

'Let's hope it's a big hit with mine! So, what do you think? Shall I ask my aunt if we can use her house?'

Warily she said, 'Ian, I'd have to see it before we made definite arrangements, make sure it's suitable for both a fairground and a marquee, and there must be room for a big car park, remember?'

'You think of everything, don't you?' he said with approval. 'I wish you worked for me. None of the women who work here have your head for business.'

'Why, thank you, Ian,' she said, flushing. 'In my job you need an eye for detail. So, do you think I could come out there some time this weekend? I'm going that way—we've bought this cottage out near Castle Howard and I'm dropping in there on Saturday to walk round it with a builder. After I've talked to him I could come on to your aunt's house.'

'That's an excellent idea; I'm sure my aunt will take to you. She likes intelligent women.'

She laughed. 'This is my day for compliments, isn't it? What time shall I get there?'

'Could you make it by four? We could have tea with Aunt Flora.'

'Flora—what a lovely name.'

'Yes, and I mustn't get confused . . . I don't want to mix my Flora up with my Laura, do I?' This amused him a lot, but when he had stopped laughing he gave her directions for the house and

Laura wrote them down, getting slightly confused after a moment or two.

'Hang on, Ian... could we go over that again? You said turn left at the farm, right by the pond and then left again...'

'No, left by the pond and then right...' Ian paused, then said, 'Look, shall I come and pick you up on my way? I shall be driving past the Castle Howard road. It wouldn't be much of a detour.'

Laura had been dreading the thought of driving around Yorkshire all afternoon looking for his aunt's house, and was relieved by this offer of a lift, but felt she had to say politely, 'Are you sure?'

'Certain,' he said with a trace of amusement in his voice. 'I'll take you there and bring you back to your cottage to pick up your car again. Now, where exactly is your cottage?'

The directions to the cottage were much easier; Ian said he would find it without a problem, and promised to arrive at three-thirty, then rang off.

Laura scribbled a note to herself: she had to find a caterer for a medieval banquet and a marquee in which to hold it.

She had hardly done so when her secretary buzzed her to say that the new client had arrived. Telling Anne to show him in, Laura stood up behind her desk, a warm smile ready, holding out her hand as he walked into the room.

'Hello, Mr Ames. How are you?'

She detached her mind from thoughts of Ian Eyre's medieval fair, and gave all her considerable concentration to the affairs of her new client. By the time he left it was half-past four and Laura was mentally tired. She signed a pile of letters Anne brought her, then they checked over the diary for next week. Laura dictated a rapid memo about the need to book a marquee for the fair and find staff to work on the banquet, then another memo on the subject of the new client's requirements.

Leaning back in her chair, she yawned, putting a hand over her mouth. 'Aah…sorry, Anne, I think I've had enough for one day. I'm going home. Put those memos into the computer, then you can go too.'

Anne nodded and vanished back to her own office and by the time Laura was leaving Anne had already almost finished keying the memos into the computer.

'Have a good weekend,' Laura said, pausing to watch her secretary's rapid fingers.

'Thanks. And make sure you get a good rest; you look tired,' Anne said, breaking off to look up at her with concerned eyes.

Laura grimaced. 'I've got a lot to do this weekend. I've got to drive to our new cottage, and then over to Ian Eyre's aunt's house, but thanks for the thought.'

'At least you won't be in the office, you'll be out in the fresh air,' Anne said, fingers poised over the computer keys. 'A change is as good as a rest, after all.'

As she drove to her flat Laura remembered the cliché, thinking wryly how true the words were, however glibly spoken. Her visit to Paris had been a wonderful rest, although she had walked for hours with Patrick around the city. Her body had been tired, but it had been a pleasant glow of weariness as she fell into bed each night after a warm bath.

She hadn't felt, as she did now, that her brain was racing like an overheated car engine and wouldn't give her any peace or let her sleep. She was both exhausted and hyperactive—a lethal combination.

She stopped to buy food for the weekend, a chore she had to do for herself now that Patrick was away. His absence was teaching her how much she had come to rely on him for day-to-day comfort—the flat was no longer immaculate, she would have to do some housework this weekend, she had to do her own cooking as well as shopping, and there was a pile of unattended laundry in her bathroom basket. She would have to do some washing and ironing, too.

The flat seemed cold and empty without him. She unpacked the food, put it all away, then sorted out washing and put it into the machine before deciding what she would eat that evening. She was too tired to cook an elaborate meal, so she simply had a salad with grilled sole.

Later she hoovered the flat and polished the furniture, then did a few other chores before she finally went to bed, only to wake up some time during the night from a strange, vivid dream about the cottage. She had been alone there, at night, but kept hearing sounds, footsteps, creaking floorboards. She ran from room to room, heart racing in panic, cold sweat pouring down her face.

The final room she entered was the main bedroom; it was full of silvery moonlight, but there was a dark shape by the window, a man standing there in shadow. He moved forward and the moonlight fell across his face. It was Josh Kern. Laura began to tremble.

He stared at her, mockery in his dark face. Laura couldn't move, she could only stare back, and as she did so her mouth began to burn. Jerkily, she put a hand up to it, while he watched her. Her fingers slowly slid along her lips, feeling the imprint of his mouth there, as if he had only just kissed her, and Josh Kern began to laugh.

Laura woke up, his laughter still ringing in her ears. Dazedly she switched on the light beside her bed and sat up, shuddering. Why on earth was she dreaming about *him*?

She slid shakily out of bed, only just able to walk, caught a disturbing glimpse of her flushed face, her fevered eyes, in the mirror, looked hurriedly away and went to make herself some hot chocolate.

She sat up in bed for a while, drinking the chocolate, reading a book to take her mind off her dream, before lying down and going back to sleep.

She must be overworked. Nothing else could explain it. The last person on earth she wanted to dream about was that man!

She got to the cottage next day to find the builder already there, wandering around the garden. He wasn't alone, though. Josh Kern was with him, and at the sight of him, in crisp new blue jeans and a polo-neck white sweater, his black hair smoothly brushed down, Laura's heart jumped like a fish out of water and she felt a pulse beating hard in her throat.

'Good afternoon, Miss Grainger,' said the builder cheerfully, grinning as she joined them. 'We're lucky with the weather today—no wind, and it isn't raining, so I've been able to go up on the roof with Josh here to hold my ladder for me. Thought I would get on with it before you arrived, save your time as well as my own. The news is good—there's only a couple of days' work to be done up there. Nothing serious wrong at all.'

'Well, that's a relief, Mr Hudson,' she said, ignoring Josh Kern's insistent grey stare. Judging by his clothes, he hadn't been working on any nearby field, so why was he here, just when she was meeting the builder?

Mr Hudson beamed at her. 'I'm sure it is, miss! And while we were at it, we walked all round the outside. Not much wrong there, either, although one of the window frames is rotten—that's got to be replaced—and you really should have the cottage repainted. Mind you, even that isn't urgent—you could leave that until next year—so you aren't looking at much work, after all.'

'That's great news.' She smiled back brightly. 'I shall have to consult my fiancé about the painting. I expect we shall want it done this summer, when the weather's good.'

'Aye, that'd be favourite!' He nodded.

'Right. Well, if you've seen the exterior, shall we go inside now, Mr Hudson?'

She didn't look at Josh Kern, hoping that he would take a hint from her distant manner, and leave.

He didn't. She had known he wouldn't, hadn't she? He wouldn't be here at all if he didn't intend to stay, driving her crazy merely by being there.

She unlocked the front door and he followed her and Mr Hudson into the cottage, and short of being openly rude to him there was nothing Laura could do about getting rid of him. He walked around with them as if he was involved in the decision-making: listening and indeed commenting freely on what the builder said, and Mr Hudson deferred to him and agreed with him, consulting him rather than Laura whenever he was suggesting what he felt should be done, as if Josh Kern still owned the cottage. Laura managed to hang on to her temper, somehow, but she was seething inside, and underneath the anger surged a very different emotion, just as explosive, but far more deadly.

She kept remembering the last time they had met, the feel of his mouth against her own, the touch of his hands, and the piercing excitement she had felt, the aching desire to put her mouth against his skin and absorb him through every pore.

Hot colour burned in her face every time she remembered, and she tried not to meet Josh Kern's eyes in case he saw something of what she was thinking about.

When Mr Hudson left, twenty minutes later, she turned on Josh, her green eyes brilliant with fury.

'What are you up to? How did you come to be here so opportunely, just when I was meeting Mr Hudson? And don't tell me you were working in the next field because I can see you weren't; your clothes . . . and you . . . are much too clean!'

He laughed. 'Aren't you observant! No, I knew you'd be here because Alf Hudson told me so when I ran into him earlier in town, and as I was driving back I saw him struggling to put a ladder up against the wall so...'

'So you thought you'd got a good excuse for turning up again and making my life difficult!' she snapped, and he put on an air of baffled innocence.

'I was only being a good neighbour, giving Alf a hand!'

Laura eyed him with disfavour. 'Come off it! You used Mr Hudson as an excuse—don't try to kid me! I know you're playing games to try to chase us away. Every time I come here I find you turning up. Well, whatever you're up to you can stop it! You aren't scaring me off, or putting me off; I am buying this cottage and I intend to move in here, whatever you do, so I advise you to stop wasting time with your little games, Mr Kern, and just get used to the idea!'

He listened with his head slightly on one side, watching her with that cool grey stare unchanged by her angry voice.

When she stopped talking there was a little silence. Very flushed, she waited for him to say something, but when he did it was not in reply to what she had said, but was so much at a tangent that it took her completely by surprise.

'Are you getting married before you move in?'

Laura stared. 'What?'

'Are you getting married before you move in here?' he repeated while she tried to work out what was behind the question.

'Probably, but we haven't decided on a date yet!'
Why did he want to know? What new scheme had
come into that corkscrew mind of his?

Softly he murmured, 'Alf Hudson said something about your fiancé not coming along today
because he was abroad at the moment. Is he going
to be away for long?'

'No, he isn't,' she said shortly, the hairs on the
back of her neck prickling. She didn't want to talk
about Patrick to this man. An atavistic instinct
buried deep inside her kept warning her that Josh
Kern was dangerous to her. He was a predator,
hunting for prey—keep away from him! that little
voice kept telling her, and she would, if she could,
but how could she when he kept turning up every
time she came here?

He arched his brows, watching her with that in-
furiating little smile. 'No? Alf seemed to think he
would be travelling around Europe for months.'

'You and Mr Hudson did have fun, didn't you,
gossiping together about my personal life?' Laura
muttered, very flushed. 'I shall have to be careful
what I say to him in future!'

Josh Kern laughed aloud. 'Oh, come on! He
hardly revealed state secrets! I asked if your fiancé
would be with you and Alf said no, you would be
on your own, because your fiancé was abroad!
What's wrong with that? Alf Hudson has known
me most of my life; he knows I'm not some crimi-
nal who might use private information to burgle
the house, or break in while you're here all alone,
and...' He broke off, his mouth twisting mock-

ingly. 'And do whatever it is you're afraid I might do.'

Their eyes tangled, and her breathing quickened. 'I didn't say I was afraid of anything!'

'You don't need to say it; I can see it,' he said softly.

'Imagination,' she muttered, but she was afraid. She just wasn't sure what she was afraid of... Yet whenever she was with Josh Kern her nerves were on edge; she was always waiting, expecting... what? She met Josh Kern's eyes and hurriedly looked away.

'You *look* afraid,' he said, suddenly very close, standing inches away from her, which didn't help to slow down her heartbeat. Laura swallowed, hoping he couldn't hear the rapid thudding which was almost deafening her.

Lifting her chin and outstaring him, she lied vehemently. 'I look angry, Mr Kern, not afraid! Now, will you leave, please?'

He looked down into her green eyes. 'That isn't anger I can see in your eyes. It's something very different; you remind me of a wild cat who lives in one of my barns. She has eyes just that green... and she spits and hisses at me if I get too close.'

'Good for her!' muttered Laura.

He looked amused. Turning his head, he pointed at the side of his neck, just under his ear. 'She uses her claws on me, too; she did this yesterday!'

Laura stared at the long, angry red scratch on his brown skin, breathing fast. 'You should be careful of that—it could turn septic,' she huskily said, fighting a stupid desire to touch it, run her fingers down that smooth brown skin. To keep her mind on other things she gabbled, 'Have you had a tetanus shot lately? You can get tetanus from an infected cat, you know.'

'Of course I know,' he drawled, watching her as if he could read her mind, a possibility that made ice trickle down her spine. 'I work on a farm. I'd be stupidly reckless if I didn't have regular tetanus shots. And if I didn't remember my mother would remind me.'

Laura was very curious about his mother, and anyway, that too was a safe enough subject, so she said, 'Mr Hudson told me that your mother was a famous cook.'

'She is.' He nodded. 'I eat like a king. But she also has her eye on everything on the farm. I wouldn't have been clawed yesterday if my mother hadn't told me to catch the little cat and take her to the vet before she was old enough to start having kittens. It took me half an hour of running around the barn before I finally cornered the creature and got her into the basket to take her to the vet, and I was furious by then, especially with my mother for sending me to do it, but it had to be done. We have enough wild cats on the farm as it is; we don't want any more.'

'You didn't have the cat put down?' Laura was distressed by that idea. She was already identifying with the little cat; she could almost see it, hissing and clawing, its hair standing on end as it was backed into a corner, and her green eyes were brilliant with sympathy.

He looked down at her and smiled suddenly, charm in his hard face for that instant. 'Good heavens, no, she'll be back, when she recovers from her operation. You can't just let cats breed naturally, even on a farm, where they can be very useful, killing vermin. We'd be overrun with them in a year or two if we didn't have most of them neutered. My mother loves cats; she has three of them living in the house, as well as the wild ones in the barns.' Josh Kern watched Laura, his grey eyes glinting with a wry humour, half veiled by lowered lids. 'I wonder what she'd think of you,' he murmured, and Laura wondered too.

She would love to meet his mother, but she was afraid Mrs Kern was going to resent her, the way Josh did.

'Does she know we're buying the cottage?'

'I've told her Dale is trying to sell it,' he evasively shrugged.

'But not that somebody has actually bought it?'

'You haven't, yet,' he said coolly. 'It will be a couple of months before the sale is completed.'

Her green eyes flashed. 'And you hope to get rid of us before then!'

That was when he took her breath away. 'No, I've changed my mind,' he murmured, and Laura stared at him incredulously.

'What?'

'I like the idea of you living in this cottage,' he said, and her heart crashed like cymbals in her chest, reverberating through her whole body and making her deaf.

'Is this another of your games?' she asked in husky uncertainty.

'I'm not playing a game,' he said, his hands remorselessly reaching for her, and she backed, shaking her head, like the wild cat in the shadowy barn, trembling yet defiant, green eyes spitting fire, running from a power she didn't understand except that it could destroy her if she didn't escape.

'Don't touch me!'

She turned to run, but he caught her, as he had caught the cat, faster and stronger than either of them. Laura had almost got to the front door when he grabbed her shoulders. He pushed her back against a wall, enclosing her with his hands on either side of her head, watching her with bright, inexorable eyes as she twisted and turned.

'Stop fighting it,' he whispered. 'You know you want me as much as I want you, Laura. Your mouth told me that when I kissed you the last time you were here. Your whole body told me; desire came off your skin, a heat I could feel with my fingertips...'

She was hot now, face burning, body burning. But she wouldn't give in, either to him or her own incomprehensible emotions. She shook her head. 'No, it isn't true; this is just another of your little games to get rid of us, make us go away...'

'I'm never going to let you go away again, Laura,' he said in a deep, harsh voice, and then his body forced itself down against her, and she felt a wave of weakness flood through her, making her shake as if she were dying, her legs almost giving under her.

Very slowly he lowered his head. She had stopped struggling; she watched his mouth come closer and closer, hypnotised, no longer able to think about anything but the hard, male strength of that mouth. It seemed an eternity before his mouth finally touched her own and, when it did, Laura shook violently, but his lips merely brushed hers, and lifted again, leaving her hungry.

'You drive me crazy,' he muttered, voice thick, moving restlessly against her, his muscled thighs pressing down, and Laura shuddered with response, and hated herself for it.

She tried to hang on to thoughts of Patrick, but couldn't conjure up a picture of him. He escaped her like mist; her thoughts dissolved every time. There was only one reality at that moment: the man touching her body softly, and watching her while he touched her, with those glittering grey eyes.

'Why can't you leave me alone?' she cried out, anguished. 'I don't want you touching me!'

'Don't lie, Laura,' he said, and his mouth descended again, gave her another brief kiss, then before she could recover gave her another, and went on tormenting her, over and over again, with light, brief kisses, catching her mouth and letting it go again only to take it once more a second later, like a cat with a mouse, teasing and playing with her until she was driven out of her mind.

She tried not to respond; she tried to think of Patrick, to remind herself she loved another man and that this unbearable sensation rising inside her had nothing to do with love, was something shameful, to be resisted. But when she looked at

Josh she couldn't think of anyone but him—his lean, hard face, his intensely sexy body.

She must not look at him! She closed her eyes so that she wouldn't see his taut, dark face; and too late realised her folly. She was out of the frying pan, into the fire. Once her eyes were shut she was plunged into a world of darkness and desire where she could at last admit the truth: that she wanted him so badly that nothing else mattered.

'I wanted you the minute I saw you,' Josh whispered, curving a hand around her breast, and she went completely to pieces, moaning with pleasure.

Her body melted, arching up to meet the force of his, and her mouth met his, parting and quivering in wild invitation. Josh made a rough, hoarse sound, then his mouth merged with hers, moving in a passionate demand that sent her helplessly into a spiral of wild, erotic excitement. The intensity was so piercing that she forgot everything but the way he was making her feel, the hot need pulsing through them both.

Until a harsh noise broke in: the blare of a horn, outside the cottage, raucous and insistent.

They jumped apart, startled: faces flushed, eyes dazed.

Josh swore. 'What the hell was that?'

Confused, Laura couldn't think. She was shuddering, her mouth hot and very pink, the sensitive tissues of her lips swollen by his kisses, her body still vibrating with desire.

The horn blared again, more urgently, and then Laura remembered. 'Ian...' she whispered, biting her lip.

Josh looked sharply at her. 'Who?'

She couldn't meet his eyes. She wanted to die. How could she have let him make love to her like that? Shame burnt in her like a red-hot iron, agonising and unbearable.

'It's someone who's come to pick me up,' she muttered, turning automatically to look into the little mirror hanging on the wall by the door. 'Oh...I look so...' She couldn't finish that sentence; it was too bitterly true. She looked like a woman who had been making passionate love. Her blonde hair was dishevelled by Josh's wandering fingers, her mouth bare, all lipstick gone, her eyes far too betraying.

'What do you mean, pick you up? You drove here in your own car,' Josh bit out, watching her with hard, narrowed eyes as she began desperately to erase the traces of her reckless passion, running a brush over her tangled curls, renewing her lipstick, dusting her skin with powder.

'Look, leave me alone...mind your own business...' she muttered, but he was already asking another terse question.

'Why are you seeing another man while your fiancé is away?'

'Oh, be quiet!' Laura snapped, resenting his tone.

In the mirror she saw his grey eyes harden, glitter with bitter distaste, and then rapid footsteps sounded outside, followed by a brisk tattoo on the door.

'Laura, are you there? Are you coming?' Ian called, and she pushed past Josh Kern and opened the door, somehow managing a bright smile although it felt stiff and phoney on her mouth.

'Sorry to keep you waiting, Ian; I was just coming!'

'I saw your car so I knew I'd come to the right place,' he said cheerfully, and slid an appreciative look over her. 'You look very elegant today, but then you always do. Are you ready? My aunt's a fanatic about punctuality.'

His face changed as Josh Kern emerged from behind her, grim and unsmiling. Ian did a double take, startled, but almost immediately pulled himself together and gave Josh a polite smile, saying smoothly, 'Hello, there! You must be the builder who's been looking at the cottage. I hope I didn't come too early and interrupt before you had finished your discussion.'

'Our discussion?' repeated Josh, smiling oddly.

Laura turned away, face hot.

Josh softly said, 'Oh, we can go on with our...' He paused, then went on in that blandly mocking tone, 'Our discussion...some other time.'

'Oh...yes...of course,' said Ian, sounding curious and a little puzzled, as if he had picked up on Josh's veiled mockery but wasn't sure what to make of it.

Laura couldn't bear any more. 'We don't want to be late, Ian,' she muttered, banged the cottage door shut behind them, and, without so much as looking at Josh, walked towards Ian's car and got in.

Ian felt he had to say something polite to Josh. 'Nice afternoon, isn't it? Almost summer now.'

Josh eyed him bleakly, and didn't reply. Ian walked towards the car, making courteous noises of farewell. He got behind the wheel, and raised his hand to Josh, who just stared back. As they drove away, Ian whistled.

'You'd know he was born in Yorkshire if you met him anywhere in the world. We breed them that way; as grim and stubborn as our moors or our dry-stone walls.'

Laura didn't answer; she was staring at the flowing green hillsides around them, watching sheep grazing the heights, a lark hanging above the cornfield. She felt sick, remembering what had just happened. Since she'd met Patrick she had never once been tempted to be unfaithful to him. Until now.

CHAPTER FIVE

THE week Laura was supposed to meet Patrick in Amsterdam he rang her at home on the Tuesday, sounding breathless and agitated.

'Laura . . . there's a problem . . . I'm afraid I can't get to Holland this weekend. Rae wants me to spend more time in Italy. She wasn't happy with the stuff I did from Rome; I have to go back there tomorrow and have another shot.'

'Oh, no!' she groaned, turning a little pale. 'What a nuisance! Couldn't you do that and still get to Amsterdam for the weekend? I was really looking forward to it. It seems ages since I saw you.'

'I'm sorry, Laura,' he said, his voice faint and far-away, sounding oddly unlike him. 'I can't. . . no time . . . impossible . . .'

'You sound tired,' she said, concerned, because it was so unlike him to talk in that weary voice, and heard him sigh.

'It's a tiring trip. What about you? Busy at your end? How's the Eyre-York project going?'

'Fine; everything is in hand. Patrick, I am sorry about these problems with the illustrations; is this author being an absolute pest?'

'No, she's probably right about the Rome sketches; I wasn't happy with them myself,' he said flatly, adding almost in the same breath, 'How about the cottage? Any developments there? When are the lawyers going to be ready to complete?'

'Oh, a month or two at least.'

'How about this builder? We haven't told him to start work yet?'

'Of course not; we can't, legally—not until the house is ours.'

'Of course,' Patrick said, sounding relieved, and she wondered if he was worried about money—how much was this European trip costing him? The publisher was supposed to be paying for the hotels and flights, but no doubt Patrick was spending a lot, too, and would only be reimbursed at some later stage.

'Is there a problem, Patrick...?' she began to ask him, but he interrupted her hurriedly.

'I don't have time to talk, Laura. Must go. Don't worry about cancelling your flight or the hotel; that will be done for you. Sorry about the weekend. Talk to you soon.'

The phone clicked and he was gone, and Laura hung up, too, slowly, her face a battleground for conflicting emotions. Ever since Josh Kern had made love to her at the cottage, she had been scared. She urgently needed Patrick; she needed to be with him, remind herself she loved him, that they belonged together.

She looked across the room at a photo of herself and Patrick together in the garden of her parents' home. They were both laughing, their faces full of happiness; he had his arm around her and she was leaning on him.

'Oh, Patrick, why did you have to go away just now?' she groaned aloud, a pang of guilt shooting through her at the sight of his happy, smiling face. But what sort of love was it that couldn't stand fast against a man like Josh Kern? Shame washed through her. She bit her lip. That photo had only been taken late last summer. Life had all seemed so simple then. They had had everything mapped out, a glowing future in front of them. It hadn't entered her head to doubt her love for Patrick, and she knew he had never for an instant doubted her.

As if Patrick could have heard her thoughts, she gave the photo another guilty look. 'I don't doubt it now, darling!' she insisted huskily. 'Not for a second. I love you as much as ever! It's just that...' That what? she broke off, running her fingers through her hair in despair. 'Oh, what is the matter with me?' She couldn't answer her own questions. She didn't understand the effect Josh Kern was having on her, or like it—but she couldn't deny it.

It was as if she were under a spell, one that could wreck her life. She had to break it before it was too late, and she had relied on Patrick to do that, but now she was flung back on her own resources, left alone to deal with the contradictory jumble of her feelings. Childishly, she was furious with Patrick for leaving her alone just now, when she needed him most. If he were here, she wouldn't have been at the cottage alone, she wouldn't have met Josh Kern, he wouldn't have been able to make love to her and force her to admit she desired him.

Laura's face burnt every time she thought about it: remembered the wildness of her own sensuality, the heat and passion between them as they touched each other.

She shut her eyes, pushing the memory away. She loved Patrick! she repeated to herself, like a mantra, comforting herself with the repetition, as if that would end all doubt. It didn't, though. She couldn't help asking why she needed to keep reminding herself she loved him. There was a worrying element of whistling in the dark, wasn't there?

No, she thought fiercely. She wasn't whistling in the dark. She not only loved Patrick, she liked and admired him, something she certainly couldn't say about Josh Kern, who was everything she didn't like, let alone admire, in a man. She never had liked the domineering type, and he was a lot of other obnoxious things as well—arrogant, much too sure of himself, sarcastic... She could go on forever listing the things about Josh Kern she didn't like.

Whereas Patrick was such a wonderful man—warm, loving, sensitive. He would make a terrific husband; their lives dovetailed so perfectly, with Patrick preferring to work at home and enjoying all the sorts of jobs Laura simply did out of duty as rapidly as possible, from cleaning the house to gardening. In time Laura knew she would be earning a considerable amount, probably far more than Patrick ever would. They would have built a good life together.

Her eyes darkened and she winced. Why was she putting all this in the past tense? She hadn't changed her mind. She was still going to marry Patrick.

Then she thought grimly, maybe it was as well she wouldn't be seeing him just yet? Not, at any rate, while she was still in such a turmoil over Josh Kern. Patrick was an artist: intuitive, quick to respond to emotional situations; he would realise she was troubled, he would probe, gently, and she might say enough to give him some clue as to what was wrong. That would have hurt him—the last thing she wanted to do.

She could deal with it herself. Patrick need never know anything about all this.

After all, all she had to do was stay away from Josh Kern until Patrick came back, and that would be easy enough. If she didn't visit the cottage she wouldn't see Josh Kern.

And, in the meantime, she wasn't even going to think about him! From now on, every time the man pushed his way into her head she was going to push him right back out again, and think hard about something else.

For the rest of that week she managed to forget about Josh Kern by keeping as busy as possible. She had plenty to do anyway, with all the arrangements for the medieval fair to make.

On the Saturday she drove out to Ransoms again, the house owned by Ian Eyre's Aunt Flora, a rather formidable lady who had nevertheless been very polite to Laura, and had agreed to let them use the grounds for the medieval fair. The estate had proved to be ideal for the purpose: it already had a capacious car park, and there was a flat, smoothly grassed park which would be a perfect site for the fair and the marquee. On this second visit Laura took with her a camera so that she could take pictures to help plan the fair in advance, and measuring equipment, including an audio tape recorder so that she could measure distances and record her findings on tape for her secretary, Anne, to type up later.

The weather was sullen; spring showers came and went all day, so Laura cautiously put on green wellies and a lined waxed coat with a hood. She paid a brief courtesy visit to the house, to let Ian's aunt know that she had arrived, politely declined tea with the excuse that she was in a hurry, then set off to tramp the grounds, taking her photos from every conceivable angle.

The ground was sodden, and her boots squelched on the wet, muddy grass. She kept skidding as she paced out the ground, but she doggedly went on with her work, even when the rain began again, but eventually the spring shower turned into a heavy downpour and Laura took shelter under some trees on the far side of the park.

While she huddled there, her hood up, her back against an oak tree's broad trunk, she heard shots coming from the wood behind her, and stiffened in alarm. A moment later there was a scampering and she saw a rabbit break out from the trees, zig-zagging wildly from side to side as it ran into cover again behind some low scrub.

As it did so more shots rang out, but by then the rabbit was out of sight, to Laura's great relief. She heard movements, however, very close to her, in the wood—the snap of twigs underfoot, the rustling of grass and leaves as someone came through the brushwood edging the trees.

Agitated, she called out to the unseen huntsman, 'Hey! Hello! Watch where you're shooting!'

Whoever was coming stopped dead. Laura kept very still, too, safely protected by the oak's solid trunk, listening. The huntsman didn't answer her. After a moment the rustling began again, getting louder, nearer.

Her back against the oak tree, her hood up, Laura didn't see him emerge from the wood. The first she knew of his arrival was when a shape came through the curtain of rain, making her jump about a foot in the air.

'You should be more careful; you almost shot me!' she accused, her startled eyes taking the man in gradually: first the shotgun broken open and held over his arm, then his heavy riding mackintosh, a pale beige colour, long and full, over cord trousers pushed into dark boots.

'I had no idea anyone was there!' a deep voice said, and Laura's green eyes widened, lifting hurriedly. She gave an audible, horrified gasp as she recognised Josh Kern.

'You!' Why did he have to be here? How could she possibly guard against him when he kept turning up so unexpectedly?

His mouth twisted in sardonic amusement. 'Yes, me. What on earth are you doing standing about here in the pouring rain?'

'Working,' she muttered, staring at his gun. 'Was that you trying to kill that poor little rabbit?'

'That poor little rabbit . . . and a great many of his friends . . . have just devastated some fields of spring vegetables beyond the wood,' Josh Kern told her with impatience, glowering at her. 'There's been an explosion in the rabbit population this spring.

They're destructive little pests; we have to keep the numbers down.'

'That's just an excuse, isn't it?' she accused him, a fine strand of blonde hair blowing across her cheek, her green eyes dark with hostility. 'I bet you love shooting; you're the type to get a kick out of killing things!'

He didn't like the description of himself. His face hardened, his mouth a straight white line. He stared at her with freezing grey eyes and bit out, 'I'm a practical man, a working farmer; I don't have time for sentiment about dear little bunnies, when they're eating my crops and wrecking my livelihood.'

'Your crops?' she repeated, taken aback. 'Your farm doesn't stretch this far; it must be a good ten miles away. This is all Ransoms land. Does Lady Flora know you're shooting over her land?'

He gave her another grim, frowning stare. 'Do you think I'd be here without her permission? Lady Flora invited me over here today, to do some rough shooting in the wood for her tenant farmer, George Danby. It was his fields that had suffered from the rabbits most. Usually he'd deal with it himself, but he's had pneumonia and is still recuperating. So Lady Flora asked me over to shoot with George's son, Phil.'

Laura looked past him into the wood, but couldn't see or hear anyone else. 'Where is he, then?'

'He took all the rabbits we'd shot back to the farm. I was making my way through the wood to see Lady Flora before I went home.' His black brows arched quizzically at her. 'Which brings us back to you—what are you doing at Ransoms?'

'I told you—working,' she said brusquely, then, meeting those hard eyes, had to expand, 'Taking photos and measuring the ground because we're planning a publicity show here later in the summer.'

He looked incredulous. 'And Lady Flora agreed? She doesn't usually let her estate be used for that sort of public stunt.'

Laura hesitated, then said shortly, 'Ian Eyre is the client holding the publicity show.'

His eyes narrowed, hard as flint. 'Ian Eyre,' he said slowly. 'Of course—Lady Flora's nephew. I had a feeling I'd seen him before, the other day at the cottage, but I hadn't seen him for years.'

A flush crawled up her face at the reminder of the other day, of what had happened between them. Without answering, she despairingly looked at the rain coming down in sheets around them. It wasn't going to stop. It might not stop for hours, and she could not stay here with him, of all people, for company.

She slung her camera case over her shoulder, pushing her little audio recorder into the pocket of her coat, and gave Josh a fleeting look.

'I must go,' she said, poised to run back to where she had left her car.

She hadn't taken a step when there was a great white flash which split the sky. Laura jumped with a cry of panic, almost dropping her camera case. She grabbed at the case with trembling hands; she was not a nervous girl, in general, but she was frightened of thunderstorms. They had an unpredictability she feared; the noise, the flashes of white light came when you weren't expecting them.

'You aren't scared of lightning, are you?' asked Josh, face astonished.

'Yes,' she muttered reluctantly, shivering as they heard a slow, deep rumble of thunder.

'You city girls are scared of your own shadows! If you understood nature you wouldn't get so jumpy.' He grimaced, then, as another flash came and she gave another gasp, he added, 'It's too dangerous under here, you know. This oak's the highest tree in the park. If lightning hits it we could go with it.'

Laura gave him a panic-stricken look. 'We'd better run back to the house, then, before the storm gets here!'

'It's too far. There isn't time; we'd be stranded out in the open!'

The sky was split open again with a jagged streak of white light.

Laura put her hands over her eyes, shuddering. A second later she felt Josh Kern grab her by the waist.

'Wh . . . what . . . ?' she began, then gave a cry of shock as she was lifted off the ground, slung like a sack of potatoes over Josh's broad shoulder.

'Put me down!' she yelped, and he gave her a light pat on her behind as he shifted his gun slightly before he began to run.

'Stop squawking, woman. I'll put you down when we're under cover in the wood. We'll be safer there. And stop kicking your feet like that; it hurts.'

'Good!' she threw at him as they left the shelter of the oak's spreading branches of frilly green leaves, and moved into the low trees and scrub fringing the wood.

Josh loped easily, despite her weight over his shoulder, through high, wet grass, bramble patches, gorse already in yellow bloom, under interwoven branches of hazel, silver birch, hawthorn.

A little way into the wood he stopped, still holding her, his breathing slightly faster than normal; she felt him lean his gun against a tree, then he let her slide to the ground, his hands lightly controlling her as she came down.

It wasn't merely that she felt his hands touch every inch of her—her legs, thighs, hips, her waist, her breasts—although that was disturbing enough. No, it was worse than that. Their bodies were in contact all the way, close and warm contact as she slithered down, helpless to do anything about it. Laura was horribly aware of their intimacy, especially as she had to clutch at him to keep herself upright for a second or two.

'We should be safe here!' Josh said, and, breathless, she struggled free, glaring up at him.

'Safe! I wish I could believe I was! But I never feel safe around you!'

His brows shot up, his grey eyes mocking. 'Now there's a fascinating admission!'

Her face very flushed, she wished she could call the words back, but it was too late. In blurting out the truth she had given him a weapon he could use against her.

Furious with herself, she darted past him, intending to run back to her car, but Josh caught her by the waist and wouldn't let her go, laughing softly.

'No, you don't! Where are you going to, Laura? You aren't running away, are you? I'd have sworn you weren't a coward!'

That got under her skin and she faced him again, green eyes glittering. 'I'm no coward!'

'Then why were you running away?' he asked in that soft, dangerous voice, watching her in a way that made her lift her head defiantly, her blonde hair escaping in wild, wet tendrils from under the hood of her coat.

'I'm not!' she muttered, and was then compelled to stay, in spite of an awareness of the dangers of being alone with him in that wind-blown green wilderness.

She could still feel her body trembling, vibrating, from that slow, intimate contact with his as he had lowered her to the ground inch by inch, his hands rippling over her and sending heat through her veins with every touch.

'I'm just...in a hurry...have to get home...' she mumbled.

'These spring storms don't last long, and if lightning does strike it will hit that oak, or another of the bigger trees, so you can stop shaking!' Josh murmured, smiling at her in a way that made her heart turn over, which scared her even more, because she didn't want to feel this way about him.

While she was staring up at him, confused and bewildered, the lightning flashed again and, shivering, she leapt back, deeper into the shadows cast by the tangle of branches.

Josh came too and leaned his back against a wild crab-apple tree only a head taller than himself and beginning to blossom in delicate pink and white clusters of petals. His weight made the tree quiver and a few petals floated down on to his wet black hair.

Laura giggled suddenly, half hysterical. 'You have apple blossom on your hair!' she explained at his glance of surprise. 'It looks like confetti!'

He bent his head. 'Brush them off, then.'

She was dry-mouthed at once, both wanting to touch him and reluctant to feed that feeling, yet how could she politely refuse? Hurriedly she brushed the petals away, deeply aware of his wet black hair under her fingers, feeling it cling to her skin as if magnetised, feeling strange electric sparks flying between them.

Laura swallowed and moved a few steps, stood watching rain trickle from leaf to leaf of a silver birch—clear, shining drops which hung on the ends of twigs briefly before dropping with a splash into the long grass. The intimacy of being there, alone with him, in the wood, with the storm raging outside and the wind and rain making their isolation complete, made her all the more intensely aware of him, so that she did not dare risk looking in his direction.

'So what exactly is this publicity stunt you're planning?' he asked, and she seized on the chance to talk about something impersonal.

'Every year Ian Eyre's company put on some event to launch their latest textile designs,' she coolly said, her voice becoming businesslike. 'Buyers come from all over the world to see what they're doing, and Ian likes to give them something special, impress them—woo them, if you like—so that they'll give him big orders for the next season's materials.'

'What a performance! Just to sell his textiles? Why can't he simply show the buyers his new designs without all this carry-on?'

'It's the way big business operates these days,' Laura told him. 'To sell you need to make an impact! Anyway, we've been handling the Eyre-York account for several years now, and we always try to come up with a striking...' she paused, selected a new word carefully '...no, a unique idea! Ian expects us to come up with something very different each time, to beat his competition.'

Josh eyed her, his mouth crookedly cynical. 'And what have you come up with this year?'

'A medieval fair...' she began, and he interrupted.

'What?' And he laughed. 'You're not serious!'

Flushed, she said crossly, 'Perfectly serious, and Ian Eyre loves the idea!'

'He would,' Josh said, face wry. 'The man was always a pompous idiot, even when he was young. Do you mean to tell me Lady Flora gave you permission to have the fair at Ransoms?'

'Yes, she did!' Laura resented his derisive expression.

'She must be going out of her mind!'

'On the contrary, Lady Flora knows a good idea when she hears it! And she's a shareholder in Eyre-York!'

'Oh, well, that explains it—she would do the dance of the seven veils in the park for money!'

'That's not a very nice thing to say about her! And she didn't strike me as the mercenary type, either.' Laura gave him an indignant stare. She had been impressed by Lady Flora, who was a strong-minded old woman with a powerful personality.

He shrugged. 'I didn't say she was mercenary, it's just that she needs every penny she can get to pay for the upkeep of that great barn!'

They could just see the house through the trees—twisting red barley-sugar chimneys, dark red brick and black timbering, faded pink tiles on the roof. Ransoms was very old; the central part of the house had been built in the fourteenth century, the two wings added on each side during the reign of Queen Elizabeth, giving the house the required E shape fashionable at that time as a polite compliment to the monarch.

'It will make the perfect backcloth for our fair,' Laura said with a sigh.

Josh considered the house, too. 'I suppose it will. What exactly do you mean by medieval fair? Is it something special, or will you just have people in medieval dress on the stalls?'

'No, it's more than that. We're trying to make it as authentic as possible—a maypole, with a local folk-dance group dancing round it, swings and merry-go-rounds, jugglers, fire-eaters; I've got someone making gingerbread men to sell, and one stall will sell pomanders...that's oranges stuck with cloves, hanging on ribbons... Medieval people used them to keep nasty smells at bay.'

'And they believed they kept disease at bay, too,' he drily said. 'I do know something about old customs!'

'Sorry, I didn't mean to sound patronising!' Laura gave him an irritated look. Why did he have to be so difficult? 'We're also having a medieval banquet served to the guests, in a marquee, after we've had the fashion parade in there,' she added. 'That's why I'm here, to work out the exact details of where to site each stall, each attraction, the rides and games, and so on. Not forgetting the marquee; the site for that has to be selected very carefully because we'll need it near the house, of course, to make it easier to bring food, china, glass et cetera out and take it back to the kitchens.'

'All this just to sell some cloth!'

'It could bring in orders worth millions!'

'Hmm,' he drawled. 'There's going to be a lot of local curiosity about it; will you let the public in?'

She looked taken aback. 'Oh, no! We couldn't do that. This is strictly a business affair, invitation only.'

Josh gave her a dry look. 'You may have a problem keeping local kids out.'

She got her notepad out of her bag and made a hurried note. 'I must talk to Ian about that; something will have to be done—maybe we can have security staff to patrol the grounds.' She put away her pen and pad and looked up to meet a cool, direct stare from his grey eyes.

'You may be scared of lightning, but you can be very tough about other things, can't you?' he murmured. 'A few minutes ago you were very shocked by the idea that I shot rabbits, but you aren't going to let a few kids spoil your important business venture. What will your security staff do about the kids? Chuck them out, or shoot them?'

Scarlet flowered in her cheeks. 'Don't be ridiculous! If the locals see that the place is patrolled and there are signs saying the fair is private they'll keep out!'

'And if they don't?'

She was irritated. 'We'll deal with that when we get to it. I'll talk to Ian about it first.'

His eyes narrowed. 'See a lot of him, do you?'

'I told you! My firm does his publicity and public relations.' Laura was very conscious of hidden meaning in his question, in the cynical curl of his mouth.

'Why do you always answer a question with an evasion?'

'I don't know what you're talking about!'

'Oh, yes, you do. What does your fiancé think about you seeing so much of Ian Eyre? Or doesn't he know anything about it?'

She was incensed by the implication, but she tried to hold on to her temper because she sensed it would be dangerous to lose control of herself in any way while she was alone with this man. The only way she could defend herself against him was to maintain a cool façade, to keep him at a distance both physically and emotionally.

'Patrick and I don't have secrets from each other!' she said with every appearance of calm. 'He trusts me and I trust him!'

His grey eyes gleamed mockingly. 'Have you told him I kissed you at the cottage the other day?'

She couldn't keep up the pretence of being cool much longer; her eyes slid away, her pulses beating violently at throat and wrist as the memory of those moments in his arms came back. She couldn't have said a word to save her life.

'So you didn't,' Josh said softly, and Laura felt a rush of anger as she heard the satisfaction in his voice.

'I'd forgotten all about it!' she snapped, and he stopped smiling and gave her a dark stare, eyes hard as flint.

'Liar!'

She held her head up, her face tense and defiant. 'It didn't mean anything; I've had passes made at me before by men I couldn't stand—most women get that, at one time or another... It wasn't important!'

'Oh, wasn't it?' he asked through his teeth and took a long stride towards her. Laura panicked and began to run, but skidded on the muddy path, and fell headlong into the long, wet grass. Before she could recover from the fall she felt his hands fasten on her waist and lift her, turning her over. Dazed, she looked up at him through a flurry of dishevelled blonde hair.

'Did you hurt yourself? Are you OK?' he asked, and she shook her head, unable to speak.

No, she was not OK. She was hurting badly. Her fall had given him the chance to touch her again, and all her defences were down. The walls had tumbled and the sea flooded in; she was overwhelmed by sudden, unbearable desire.

He was kneeling beside her, supporting her on one arm. She made no effort to get up, or get away. Their eyes held; she was drowning in the intensity of his gaze, reading her own emotions in his dilated pupils. The savagery of the storm—the wind, the rain, the crash of thunder—was forgotten as the world shrank to this small circle in which the two of them confronted each other.

She heard quick, husky breathing and didn't know if it was her own, or his; it didn't matter. Nothing mattered but the satisfying of her terrible, driving need. He lowered his head and her mouth lifted, parted, yielding and hungry as his lips came down in that insistent demand.

Her eyes closed involuntarily. She didn't want to see or hear anything; she wanted to shut out the world, enclose the two of them in this deep, velvet silence where their mouths clung and their bodies arched to meet, needing to touch, to merge.

She was shuddering as if she was icy-cold, and yet she was burning with a terrible fever, and his mouth was hot; urgent. Without taking it from hers, Josh fumbled with the buttons on his heavy mackintosh and pulled her closer, inside it, into the warmth of his body. Laura's hands stole like mice inside his tweed jacket, undid his shirt enough to nest against his bare skin, exploring the hollows under his ribs, following the line of bone, the knot of muscle, feeling the beating of his heart under her fingers, the roughness of hair growing down to his midriff.

His hands were busy, too; he had undone her own coat, had his hands inside it, pushing her closer, moulding her into the curve of his body, caressing her hair, letting the damp coils of it fall through his fingers before pushing his fingers underneath to stroke her nape in a strangely intimate, gentle movement which made her groan with pleasure. His fingertips trailed down her throat, setting her pulses beating even faster; she didn't even protest when he unzipped the sweater she wore, and when his hands covered her silk-covered breasts she only moaned.

He slid his arms right round her then, still kissing her, and pulled her closer so that their bodies touched, bare skin against bare skin, the rain pouring down over their heads, the earth wet under them, the grass hissing and murmuring as they moved on it with such restless urgency.

For the first time in her life Laura experienced a desire so fierce it was like being ripped apart; she was aching inside; the deep, drugging exchange of kisses only tantalised and deepened that ache.

She felt her jeans give way as Josh unzipped them; a groan broke from her as his cool fingertips crept down, inside her panties, touched her thighs, between them, where the heat was more intense.

'No,' she gasped thickly, and Josh lifted his head, breathing harshly, roughly.

Laura tried to open her own eyes, but they were as heavy as lead; or was it just that she did not want to open her eyes, let the world break in on them?

If she opened her eyes she would have to face the truth about the way she felt, she would have to think—and she didn't want to think. She wanted to stay in that secret, passionate world forever, this place where there was just the two of them and this wild, sweet feeling beating between them.

'Yes,' Josh muttered, his hands busy again, making her shudder with sensuality. She felt her jeans go, cold air touch the heated flesh; she should stop him now. She must stop him. She tried to break out of the spell holding her. She could only cry silently, tears trickling through her lashes.

'Don't,' Josh said. 'Don't cry.' And his tongue touched her lids, gently, so gently, licking the tears from her lashes. But at the same time he was kicking off his boots, his body moving hurriedly, out of the rough cord trousers; then he was on top of her, naked, covering her from the wind and rain, the rough pressure of his thighs forcing her back into the grass, his hands under her, lifting her, opening her legs.

Laura felt as if she was ringed with fire: as if the world were on fire around her, within her; and as the hard, driving thrust of his body came down on her and entered her she cried out in a wild voice, an almost inhuman voice. The flames leapt up with him, inside her body, burning and melting her, and her arms went round him, her body arched to meet him.

Now she met his movements with an erotic intensity which made Josh groan; their bodies rose and fell together, becoming one and parting, only to come together again, the sound of their breathing faster and rougher, the spiral of tension wound higher and higher until she was on the point of screaming. Her head twisted and turned against the long, wet grass; her mouth open in a moan of passion, a primitive mask of female desire changing her utterly, stripped now of her cool smile, her self-control, her efficiency, Laura was another creature, a woman possessed. Josh heard the note in her voice change, raised his head and looked at her once, his eyes fierce, his face hot, his breathing tortured, then he let himself come into that wild ecstasy too, his cries of unbearable satisfaction mingling with hers.

For a long time after that neither of them moved. Josh's wet head lay against her naked breasts, pillowed and heavy, his legs between her thighs, the warmth slowly evaporating from her.

At last he lifted his head. 'Now tell me that wasn't important!' Josh said thickly. 'Tell me you'll be able to forget all about that!'

Laura desperately wished she could. She shuddered a sigh, forced at last to open her eyes. They were wet with tears, their green darkened in pain.

'It can't be important; it mustn't be!' she whispered. 'It's just a moment of madness; it doesn't mean anything... I love Patrick; I'm going to marry him...'

His face was hard, insistent. 'If you do, you'll only regret it, and so will he, because you'll be marrying him while you want me.'

CHAPTER SIX

LAURA couldn't bear any more. She pushed him away, struggled up, dressed, her fingers clumsily fumbling with her damp, crumpled clothes, her back to him as he got up, too, and dressed again. Without looking at him again, Laura fled from the wood, discovering almost with shock as she emerged from the trees that it was no longer raining; the sky was a clear, rain-washed blue and a rainbow arched in the distance, shimmering.

She hadn't even noticed the moment when the lightning ceased to flash, the thunder to roll, the rain to fall. She probably wouldn't have noticed the earth open or a volcano erupt while Josh was making love to her! she angrily thought, heading towards the house.

She was almost halfway there when she heard him behind her. Josh wasn't running. He was walking, the sound of his footsteps magnified by the wet grass he trod down; nevertheless he began to gain on her. His legs were longer, his strides covered a lot of ground. Laura felt like someone being tracked by a remorseless hunter; her nerves jumped and leapt and her heart raced. She had to get away from him.

She was out of breath by the time she got to her car. She was in such a hurry that she dropped her keys, scrambled for them, then dropped her camera.

She felt like swearing; she wanted to yell and
scream. What was the matter with her? She used
to be calmly efficient, a modern woman who could
deal with her life without a problem, capable of
coping with any crisis. Now she seemed to be
coming to pieces, and it was all his fault! Josh Kern!
she thought, shaking with rage. Her life had been
fine until he showed up in it!

Josh caught up with her as she finally got her
car key into the lock.

'No, you don't!' he ground out between his teeth,
grabbing her by the shoulder to stop her getting
behind the wheel. 'Running away won't solve
anything!'

She turned on him, green eyes spitting fire. 'For
God's sake, leave me alone!'

'You can't go ahead and marry him now! Do you
think he'd want to marry you if he knew you didn't
love him?'

'I do!' she cried, almost desperate, struggling to
get away.

'No, Laura. You know that isn't true. Stop lying
to yourself!'

Her face dissolved into a confusion of obstinacy
and uncertainty, her green eyes wild, her lips trembling, her chin lifted in defiance—she no longer
knew what was the truth and what was not, but
she was not going to let him order her around as
if she were a child. This maelstrom swirling around
inside her made it impossible to know for sure how
she really felt about anything, so she clung to the
only comfort she had left.

'I love Patrick, and I'm going to marry him!'

Josh stared down at her. 'I suppose you think that if you say that often enough it will come true? Well, it won't, Laura. You may have thought you loved him, once, but that was before you met me!'

His assurance took her breath away. She looked at him helplessly, longing to break down in tears, but afraid of any sign of weakness in front of him because it would give him the chance he was waiting for, betray her to him.

So she took shelter in raging at him. 'Oh, you...I suppose you think you're God's gift to women! That's what this is all about, isn't it? Your ego! You believe you only have to give a woman a smile and she's ready to fall at your feet! Well, I've got news for you, Mr Kern—your wonderful charm doesn't work where I'm concerned.' Her voice rose; she was breathless and shaking with emotion she could barely hold in check but had to hide from him. 'In fact,' she wound up shakily, 'in fact, I can't stand the sight of you!'

As she stopped talking and stood there, breathing unsteadily, she heard footsteps and voices. Two women had just walked out of the heavy oak front door of the house. Laura realised with horror that if she could hear them the new arrivals must have been within earshot of her and Josh for a moment or two, and had probably heard everything she had just said.

Josh had heard them too. He let go of Laura and swung round, his body tense. Laura's first instinct was to dive past him into her car and drive away, but one of the women was Lady Flora.

Laura had been brought up to be polite, especially to her elders and betters. She couldn't have ignored Lady Flora, even if it hadn't been essential to her current project to maintain a friendly relationship with the owner of Ransoms.

While she was forcing a smile into her flushed face, the woman standing beside Lady Flora walked towards them.

'Is something wrong, Josh?' she asked, staring at Laura in obvious astonishment.

Laura wished a hole would open up and swallow her. She had never seen the woman before, but presumably she was one of the Eyre family, which, Laura knew, was a large, sprawling one with offshoots all over the north of England.

'Just our new neighbour arguing with me again, Mother,' he drily said, and Laura's eyes widened.

Mother? This was his mother? She gave Mrs Kern a longer, more searching look, and met a curiosity just as open.

Mrs Kern must be in her fifties, surely, if she was the mother of Josh Kern, who was undoubtedly over thirty, yet she didn't look it. In fact, she didn't look more than ten years older than her son. She wasn't wearing make-up of any kind and yet her skin was smooth and unlined—the skin of a much younger woman. Her dark hair was cut short, and Laura guessed the curl in it was natural. She had blue eyes, direct and frank and curious, with a distinct glimmer of humour in them. A wide mouth, long, straight nose, flat cheekbones—it was a striking face, and Laura picked up a resemblance between her and Josh.

Josh introduced them offhandedly. 'Mother, this is Laura Grainger, who has bought the cottage.'

Very pink, Laura held out her hand, mumbling an automatic courtesy. 'How do you do...?'

Would Mrs Kern be as hostile as her son had been the first time Laura met him? Remembering the reason why Josh resented the sale of the cottage to anyone outside the family, Laura wouldn't be surprised if his mother, too, cold-shouldered her. It wasn't personal. Laura had innocently wandered into the middle of the battleground, that was all.

It must have been painful, humiliating for Mrs Kern to discover that her husband had installed his mistress in a cottage on the farm, so close to home, especially as it would have been the talk of the neighbourhood. This was such a close-knit community; everyone knew everyone else, nobody could keep a secret for long, and Josh's father had known that he was insulting his wife publicly when he brought another woman to the farm and visited her openly like that. It must have been totally deliberate. What had his wife done to him to deserve such cruelty? Laura had wondered ever since she first heard about it. Mrs Kern must have been scarred terribly by those years, and when her husband died she must have thought that at last she could throw the other woman out of the cottage, only to get a final shock when the lawyers told her that the dead man had given the place to his mistress.

Of course, none of that was Laura's fault. She was simply buying the property from the other woman, but she wouldn't blame Mrs Kern if she refused to shake hands, refused to play the social game by being polite to someone who, however innocently, had taken over the symbol of her long humiliation.

But Mrs Kern did take her hand, did nod and give her a long, assessing glance, which Laura met rather shyly, and even smile, although it was a faint, wary, maybe even reluctant smile.

'So you're Miss Grainger. I wondered what you looked like; my son told me about you, but he never said you were so lovely.'

'Thank you,' Laura murmured, pleased with the compliment, but wondering, what *had* Josh said about her? She shot him a look and met ironic grey eyes she found unreadable. What was he thinking?

Lady Flora had joined them and was staring at Laura. 'My dear, what on earth has happened to you?'

Laura stiffened, colour flaring in her face. Did it show on her face, then? Those minutes in the wood with Josh?

'You're covered in mud!' expanded Lady Flora, however; and Laura looked down at herself and gave a horrified gasp. Her coat was crumpled, and filthy, with black streaks of mud and grass stains.

How on earth did she explain that? While she was searching her mind for some excuse Josh smoothly said, 'I'm afraid Miss Grainger only has herself to blame.'

She gave him an agitated sideways look, her green eyes full of alarm. She wouldn't put it past him to tell them precisely what had happened in the wood, and Laura didn't know how she could bear it if he did.

'It seems Miss Grainger is afraid of thunderstorms!' was actually what he said, though. 'One flash of lightning and she went into panic. Before I knew what was happening, she started to run and the next minute skidded on a patch of mud and fell—quite heavily, I'm afraid.'

She bit back a sigh of relief and caught a gleam of wry mockery in his glance. He had known she was afraid of what he might say. Laura burned with resentment—why could he read her mind so easily? How did she betray herself to him? She wished she knew. More and more she needed to be able to hide her thoughts from Josh.

'You didn't hurt yourself, I hope, Miss Grainger?' Mrs Kern asked her, looking quite concerned.

Laura shook her head, but didn't get a chance to say anything because Lady Flora had started talking, giving Laura a warm smile full of sympathy.

'I hate thunderstorms myself, my dear. When I was a child I used to get under the table until they were over.' A reminiscent gleam came into her eyes. 'There was a heavy gold chenille cloth over the table during the day, to protect the surface. It hung right down almost to the floor. It was as dark as a cave; I often used to play under there. I thought nobody knew I was there, but of course I realise now they must have done. When there was a thunderstorm I'd crouch down, covering my eyes, and wait for the noise to stop.'

'I used to do that, too,' Laura said, and they smiled at each other, but once Lady Flora had begun to talk about the past you couldn't stop her, as Laura had already discovered.

'During the Second World War I was in London once right at the start of the Blitz when an air raid started. I hid under the table that time, too. It took me right back to my childhood. Very strange.' She paused, staring at nothing, and Laura decided it was time to say goodbye.

'Well, I must be going...' she began, but Lady Flora still hadn't tired of the subject.

'While I waited for that air raid to stop, I kept remembering my mother laughing at me in thunderstorms, telling me to come out and not be so silly. She couldn't understand why I was scared. She was utterly fearless, my mother, although there's a Sargent portrait which makes her look very frail. When she was riding across country she took her horse over hedges even some of the men would back off from! A little thing like a thunderstorm didn't bother her. Yet if she found a spider in the bath she'd scream the place down!' She turned her eyes on Mrs Kern. 'We all have our weak spots, don't we, Nell?'

Mrs Kern nodded. 'It's human nature, and that Sargent portrait is my favourite of your pictures.'

'Mine, too,' said Lady Flora, then with a smile said, 'Won't you come in for tea now, Miss Grainger?'

Laura made excuses, sliding away towards her car. 'Very kind, but...must go...so sorry...thank you...' At last she managed to get behind the wheel, put the key in the ignition and turned it. There was a weak splutter. Then nothing.

Aware of the little group standing near by, watching her, Laura tried again. This time there wasn't even a splutter. Just nothing. She tried again. And again. Very flushed, raging inwardly, she felt like kicking the car.

Josh Kern strode over. 'Sounds to me as if your battery is dead. I'll take a look at the engine. When I give you the signal, try to start it again.'

He opened the car bonnet; she watched him inspecting the engine. He gave her a peremptory hand signal and she tried the ignition again; still nothing. After another couple of minutes Josh closed the bonnet, shrugged wryly at her.

'Dead as a doornail. Has it been giving you any trouble lately?'

She shook her head, grimly silent. Wasn't it just her luck? She was stranded here without a car; she would have to ring for a taxi, or ask Josh Kern for a lift.

'It could be the battery,' Josh said thoughtfully, 'or maybe rain got into the engine during that storm. I'll get a friend of mine to come out and take a look at it right away. If he can't fix it here and now, he can tow it back to his garage.'

'And you must come in and have a cup of tea while you wait,' Lady Flora said.

Unhappily Laura said, 'It's very kind of you, but really... I have to get back... Could I use your telephone to ring a taxi?'

'We'll drive you back,' Josh intervened, voice firm. 'Are you ready, Mother? Come along, then, both of you.'

'I can get a taxi...' Laura almost wailed, trying to resist his determined grip on her arm.

'Don't be ridiculous.' He opened the door of a big black Land Rover and took hold of Laura's waist. 'In you get.' He picked her up off the ground and lifted her into the front passenger-seat of the high-sided vehicle, then helped his mother up into the back seats before shaking hands with Lady Flora and getting in behind the wheel.

'My son is very bossy,' Mrs Kern drily told her, and Laura looked round, flushed and finding it hard to smile politely.

'Yes, he is,' she said through her teeth.

'Wave to Lady Flora, both of you,' was all Josh said, quite unabashed.

His mother and Laura obeyed, although Laura couldn't help asking herself why she was letting him order her around. Of course she would have made some farewell gesture to Lady Flora, and Josh's command seemed perfectly natural, but it was the tone of voice he used that bothered her. He sounded like a grown-up talking to children, and it made Laura's hackles rise.

As they drove on towards York he said, 'You aren't in a hurry, are you? I'll drop my mother back at the farm first, if you don't mind.'

Laura made a polite murmur, staring out across the green fields towards the distant blue-hazed moors. She could hardly say she did mind, in the circumstances, but she felt much safer with his mother in the car, and wished she had insisted on getting a taxi.

She had never been to Kern House before, although she had seen it across the fields, from the cottage. She gazed curiously at the whitewashed stone farmhouse as they drove towards it along the private road. It looked old, the walls thick, bulging faintly with age, although it wasn't a grand house like Ransoms, just a comfortable working farmhouse with outbuildings visible behind it around a large farmyard, and a well-kept garden in the front of the house.

Mrs Kern urged, 'Come in for a few moments, my dear, and have some tea.'

'She's in a hurry, Mother,' Josh curtly said, and Laura bristled.

Ignoring him, she turned to smile warmly at his mother. 'Thank you, I'd love some tea.'

Josh looked bland. 'Contrary as ever,' he drawled, leaving her wondering if he had deliberately provoked her into accepting his mother's invitation, which was a worrying possibility because it would mean that he knew her rather better than she wanted him to, and had started coolly manipulating her. Laura didn't like the thought of that at all.

He jumped down from the Land Rover and Laura scrambled out in a hurry, to avoid his help. She landed awkwardly and Josh steadied her, his arm going round her.

'You should look before you leap,' he said softly, watching the heat kindle in her face, then he walked away to help his mother down.

Laura followed them both into the farmhouse
through a side-door which led straight into a large
kitchen with an oak-beamed ceiling, whitewashed
walls and polished, well-worn, red-tiled floor. On
a dresser full of pretty china stood a huge vase of
white and purple lilac, the scent filling the room.
Mrs Kern filled a kettle and put it on the hob of a
range which filled the old farm fireplace and gave
a steady background warmth.

'I'll go and ring my garage friend, get him to
pick up your car,' Josh said, walking out.

Laura felt easier at once. 'Can I help?' she asked
as Mrs Kern began to lay the table.

'Thank you, dear. Could you get three cups and
saucers down from the dresser?'

She had never thought Mrs Kern would ever
invite her here, or be so friendly. From Josh's attitude the first time she met him Laura had expected nothing but bitter hostility from his mother.
Had the passage of time since her husband's death
made it easier for Mrs Kern to accept the fact of
other people living in the cottage where he had once
visited his lover?

She selected cups and saucers from the display
on the dresser—rose-sprigged china in a fluted
shape—laid them out on the clean white tablecloth,
where Mrs Kern had already put out a plate of
home-made scones, a bowl of home-made straw-
berry jam, a butter dish, a large rich fruit cake
which had several slices taken out of it already, a
tray set with a white bone-china sugar bowl with
silver tongs in it, a matching milk jug and finally
the large white teapot in which she had made the

tea. She slid a padded tea-cosy over this while Laura laid three plates, knives and forks, and Mrs Kern added crisply laundered white linen napkins.

'The table looks so pretty!' Laura said, standing back to admire it.

Mrs Kern looked pleased. 'I like my home to look nice, dear. It's like wearing a new dress, I always think! Gives you a wonderful lift to walk into a room that looks really comfortable and welcoming.'

'This one certainly does!' Laura took a deep breath and risked adding, 'I'm glad to have had this chance to get to meet you at last, Mrs Kern, as we're going to be neighbours. I'm sorry for the . . . the problems there have been . . . but I hope we can put all that behind us now and be friends.'

Mrs Kern gave her a grim little smile. 'Well, I've learnt to put up with what I can't change.'

Laura flinched from the flat bluntness of that.

In a gentler tone, Mrs Kern said, 'As you know, my son and I wanted the cottage back, and with good reason! It has always belonged to this family; it should never have been given to an outsider.' Her voice had a harshness that was painful to hear, then she sighed and added quietly, 'But what's done is done, and it isn't your fault; I don't hold you to blame. I hope we will be friends, lass, so sit you down, and have your tea.'

'Thank you,' Laura shyly said, obeying her. 'I haven't eaten tea for years.'

Mrs Kern gave her an incredulous look. 'You haven't? It's Josh's favourite meal.'

'Really?' That surprised Laura.

His mother sat down and poured the tea. 'Oh, aye, he enjoys his tea. He never bothers much with breakfast. He's up too early. He says he's never hungry at five in the morning.'

'No, I wouldn't be,' agreed Laura, grimacing at the very thought of getting up that early.

Mrs Kern handed her a cup and saucer. 'Help yourself to sugar if you take it, dear. No, Josh just has a slice of toast with his tea before he goes out to the milking shed, and that's it until midday, when he has his lunch, but by three-thirty or four he's starving, and he likes to sit down and have a good tea, and that keeps him going until his dinner at seven.'

Laura took a beautifully risen scone from the plate Mrs Kern offered her, split it and spread it lightly with butter while the older woman went on talking. Her son was obviously her favourite subject, and Laura was not averse to listening to her talk about him.

'He doesn't eat a big meal in the evening, mind. We go to bed early, of course, so he just has a light meal at seven—a salad and cold meat, maybe.'

The glimpse of Josh's working day was oddly fascinating to Laura, who had never lived on a farm. She wanted to know more. Questions buzzed inside her head. Did Josh read in the evenings? Watch television? Did he like pop music? Did he go out much? Did he have a girlfriend?

'Eat your scone, my dear,' said his mother, and Laura absently took a bite.

'Mmm...delicious,' she said while her mind was very much elsewhere. It had never occurred to her that there might be a woman in Josh's life. It should have done. She winced as a little niggling ache began inside her at the thought of him with someone else.

Stop it! she crossly told herself. She had no business caring whether or not Josh had another woman. It was nothing to do with her! She was engaged to someone else. Why did she keep forgetting that? Why did she keep forgetting Patrick?

Guilt flooded through her, drowning everything else. She despised herself.

She had thought her love for Patrick was so sure and unshakeable; she had planned her whole future around it; they were perfect partners. True, they were not the same sort of people, but they dovetailed together in such harmony that it had seemed totally natural, utterly right. She had always been the strong, the ambitious one. Patrick had been the gentler, more domesticated one. It had worked, that matching of opposites. She had been so certain about it, about Patrick, about a future together.

Now she was lost: confused and bewildered. The firm ground she'd thought she stood on had turned out to be quicksand.

Her eyes flashed to the door as Josh came back. Her blood began beating fast at the sight of him, as if someone had suddenly given her a jolt of electricity straight into her veins.

Just seeing him walk into a room made the whole world change for her, she thought, dazedly. As if the sun had come out on a dark day. As if winter turned into spring. As if music began in a silent room. Patrick had never once made her feel like that.

A sense of panic close to terror came over her as she admitted that. She had been trying to convince herself the way she felt wasn't serious, wasn't important, wouldn't last. It was a purely physical response to an intensely attractive man. Desire could be sated, forgotten. It could be pushed aside, ignored. It was not something a wise woman built her life on.

But what she felt for Josh was far more than desire. She hated to face that fact, but she couldn't go on hiding from the truth any longer. She didn't just want his body. It wasn't just a few crazy hormones acting up.

He had begun to matter to her. Deeply. Maybe more than anything in her life had ever mattered before.

'OK, that's fixed,' he said, and she gazed at him blankly. 'Your car,' he reminded, giving her a dry, amused look. 'The garage is going to pick it up and get it going again. I gave them your office number; they'll ring when they've done the work.'

'Oh, thank you,' she mumbled, as pink as a schoolgirl under his sardonic grey eyes. He must think she was a total idiot, not even remembering that he had been ringing the garage on her behalf!

He walked over to the sink and washed his hands, dried them efficiently on a small towel, talking over his shoulder.

'When I've had my tea I'll drive you into York.'

He came back to the table and sat down opposite her, and Laura's gaze fell. She was intensely conscious of him sitting there.

He filled the room. Her senses absorbed him: she breathed him in like a perfume, drank him like wine, tasted the excitement of his presence on her tongue; her lips, her skin, her very fingertips tingled as if they touched that lean male body. The sensations overwhelmed her. She was afraid to look at him in case he read her feelings in her eyes.

But Josh had more down-to-earth things on his mind. He reached for a scone while his mother poured his tea. Looking at Laura's empty plate, he said, 'Try a piece of cake; my mother wins prizes with her fruit cake at shows.'

'Yes, do, my dear!' Mrs Kern cut her a big slice and she protested.

'Oh, no, that's too much; less than half of that, please.'

'It is very rich,' Mrs Kern sympathised, doing as she asked and sliding the thin slice on to her plate.

Laura tasted it. 'It's wonderful!' she said in all sincerity. 'I envy you. I wish I could cook like this, but, although my mother taught me to cook, somehow nothing I made turned out too well. My pastry tastes like Plasticine and my cakes and bread don't rise.'

Mrs Kern smiled at her. 'Maybe you've never taken it seriously yet. One day you probably will and you'll find you pick it up then.'

Josh murmured, 'Any woman I marry is going

to have her work cut out matching my mother's cooking.'

There was an odd silence. Laura's face was scarlet. She felt Mrs Kern staring at her and wondered what on earth she was thinking. Josh must have told his mother that Laura was engaged, that that was why she was buying the cottage. Had he told his mother anything else? Just how much did Mrs Kern know about what had been going on between them?

CHAPTER SEVEN

LAURA found it hard to keep her mind on her work all the next week. She was too disturbed.

When he drove her back from his farm, Josh had said softly, 'Have dinner with me?' and she had shaken her head, her mouth stubborn.

He had drawn up outside her flat a few minutes later, and she had reached for the door-handle, but his hand had grabbed her shoulder, and at once she had felt the wild flare of passion his lightest touch could unleash, and trembled.

'I'm not letting you do this, Laura,' he said thickly, leaning over her to force her to look into his intent eyes. 'You have to tell him, break the engagement off, as soon as he gets back. You're not doing him any favours by going ahead with your marriage when you love me, not him.'

Anguished, she cried, 'I don't!'

'Stop lying,' he muttered, a hoarse note in his voice, his head moving down towards her. 'After what just happened...'

'Nothing happened!'

He gave her a darkly ironic look. 'You're not stupid, Laura. You know it won't help to lie about it!'

'I'm not lying. If I say it never happened, then it never happened,' she said with desperation, and pushed him away so hard that she had managed to get the door open and was out of the car before Josh recovered his balance. She didn't stop running until she was safely inside her flat with the door shut.

She got a phone call from him later that night. 'Have dinner with me,' he said without identifying himself.

'No,' Laura said, huskily.

'We've got to talk about this!'

'There's nothing to talk about!' she said and hung up.

He rang again at once, and she left the phone off the hook for an hour, but dared not leave it off any longer in case Patrick rang.

Ten minutes later the phone started again and she picked it up nervously. 'Hello?'

'I keep remembering...' Josh began, and she slammed the phone down and ran to her bedroom, threw herself on the bed, sobbing, a pillow over her head, hearing the phone begin again—a muffled sound, as if it rang underwater, like the bell of a submerged church.

She was in her kitchen making scrambled egg and toast for a late snack when there was a peremptory ring on the doorbell, and she almost answered it, but intuition warned her who was outside and she stopped dead, a hand out to turn the handle.

As if sensing her there Josh said quietly, close to the door, 'You can't keep pretending it didn't happen, Laura; we both know it did, and we've got to talk about it.'

White-faced, Laura slid silently back into the kitchen and closed the door, careful to make no sound.

Josh rang again, louder, kept his thumb on the bell for ages, banged and called her name, but eventually he went away, taking her appetite with him.

She scraped her meal into the waste-bin, and took her coffee off to bed with her.

There was a note on the mat. She was reluctant to touch it, but in the end she picked it up and read it.

I must see you. I'm not giving up so stop fighting it. I'll be back. Josh.

She crumpled it up and threw it into the bin after her wasted meal, then went to bed, but didn't sleep for hours, and when she did dreamt of Josh.

It was a relief to go back to work, but she kept drifting off into thoughts of Josh, only to be brought down to earth by a telephone ringing, or her secretary's puzzled, 'Aren't you feeling well, Laura? Or is something wrong?'

Then she would force a bright smile and briskly say, 'Wrong? No, of course not—I was just thinking. Now, where was I?'

But as soon as Anne had gone back to her own desk Laura would turn her eyes to the window and drift off again, gazing at the blue sky but seeing Josh's hard dark face.

Without her noticing it, spring had become summer; girls wore thin T-shirts with their jeans, or light summer dresses, people started going around with a tan after early summer holidays, York was even more full of tourists than usual.

At times you could hardly force your way along a pavement for the strings of visitors on their way to the cathedral or the castle, their guide talking loudly at them. Car parks and restaurants were crowded; life was impossible and Laura grew daily more depressed.

Patrick should be back soon. She held on to that, sighing whenever she got a postcard from him, or an all too brief phone call from Italy, where he seemed to be staying far too long if he had several other European capitals to visit.

'I hope the publisher is going to pay all your bills!' she said to him that week.

'Oh, he is,' Patrick assured her. 'But that reminds me—I'd better stop talking now; this call will be on his bill. See you soon, Laura.'

'Patrick, can't I come to Rome? I need to see you; I miss you,' she urgently said.

'Oh,' he said, sounding moved. 'Laura...do you? Miss me? That's...I wish you could come, too, but even if you did I doubt if I'd have time to see much of you. Rae keeps me running around the city like a cat on hot bricks; I hardly have time to breathe.'

'Why do you let her do it? I'll come to Rome; you tell her you want a couple of days off!'

He laughed. 'You make it sound so simple! The two of you are so alike, you and Rae; you're both so sure of yourselves, so hard to argue with! It's really weird.' There was a little pause, then he said hurriedly, 'Sorry, I've really got to go. Just be patient a bit longer, Laura. Talk to you again soon, bye.'

The phone clicked. He was gone. She put the phone down herself, frowning. He had seemed so odd.

Patrick had changed somehow, since going to Europe. She wasn't quite sure where the change lay, only that when they talked she felt as if he was different, a stranger to her.

No, the change is in me, she thought, biting her lip. I feel differently towards Patrick, so he seems different? But that didn't explain everything, did it? It didn't explain why Patrick's calls to her were so short and ... well, almost remote!

At first when he'd rung he'd been always loving, telling her how much he missed her, how eager he was to see her again, but over the last couple of weeks he had talked of little but the work he was doing—Rome, the places he had visited, Rome, the paintings he had seen, Rome, the impact the great artists of the past were having on him.

There was nothing personal in what he said, she realised suddenly. That was it! Patrick no longer seemed interested in her. He was only interested in what was happening to him. But he had been to Italy before. She didn't remember it making this much impact on him! He could talk of nothing else.

A sudden dart of suspicion hit her. Was it Rome Patrick was really obsessed with?

Or was it this Rae Dunhill?

The idea burst on her like a bomb exploding. She shook her head instinctively. No! The denial was almost wrenched out of her.

Not Patrick! she angrily told herself. He had never looked at anyone else. Never once since they first started dating. She trusted Patrick absolutely.

But a little voice in her head reminded, they're together all the time, judging by the way Patrick talks. Her name comes up in every other sentence. Rae said this, Rae did that... And, after all, they were alone together, in a beautiful, romantic city, miles from home.

She tried to remember everything he'd ever said over the past weeks about the writer, but couldn't think of a thing. She didn't know how old Rae Dunhill was, if she was pretty, if she was fun... She didn't know a thing about her, in fact, other than that she was successful, and that Patrick had said she was very sure of herself, and hard to argue with!

A frown drew her brows together. And he said she was like me! she reminded herself, and felt insulted. Rae Dunhill sounded like a very tough businesswoman, rather than someone creative. She obviously liked her own way and was used to getting it from Patrick.

I'm nothing like that! Laura crossly thought, then frowned. She couldn't deny that some of that description did fit her. Or had... until... until I met Josh Kern, she reluctantly admitted to herself with a sigh.

He had had a devastating effect on her. She was only just beginning to face up to it. Sometimes she caught her secretary looking at her as if she'd never seen her before, and Laura knew what Anne was thinking because she often felt when she looked into a mirror that she didn't know herself at all.

The truth was, she no longer felt sure of herself, or anything else—especially where Josh was concerned. He had knocked her off her balance and left her floundering around trying to understand precisely what had happened to her. Lately she felt helpless, bewildered, vulnerable...sensations she had never experienced in her life before.

Patrick would be as startled as Anne, no doubt, if he were here. Would he like her the way she was at the moment? Laura knew he liked those characteristics in her which he'd described as being Rae Dunhill's too. Patrick was a home-loving man who was gentle and intuitive; he needed someone stronger to twine around and that was why they had been so good together.

Oh, surely she must be imagining all this! She watched a faint white puff of cloud drift past in the summer sky, watched it as if it were an omen, could tell her whether she was right or not, could tell her what she felt.

Because now she was even more confused. She wasn't sure how she did feel about anything. Patrick and someone else? Laura had possessive instincts; she felt a stab of jealousy at the thought of Patrick with another woman. He had belonged to her for so long that she had never imagined him with someone else until now.

Yet at the same time she couldn't deny something dangerously close to relief, because if Patrick had turned to another woman then...then she was

free. But was that what she wanted? She loved
Patrick. She didn't want to lose him. Did she?

Or did she?

What was this feeling she had for Josh? She was
reluctant to put a name to it. She only knew it
couldn't be love. You didn't fall in love this fast.
What did she know about him? Only what her
senses told her, and it was dangerous to let your
senses rule your head, let alone your life.

She knew Patrick so well; there were no surprises
in their relationship any more, no new discoveries
to make about each other. There was comfort and
security in that. They would always be happy
together the way they were now, a contented couple
who dovetailed perfectly.

Of course, there was no wild excitement either.
She couldn't actually remember ever being wildly
excited over Patrick. The way she was over Josh.

That admission really hit her. She hadn't faced
up to it completely before, but now she had to. Josh
could make her feel as if her bones were melting.
The touch of his mouth made her body shake and
sent a terrible heat through her veins. Patrick had
never done that.

She was feverish instantly, remembering those
moments in the rainy wood; but she wouldn't remember... She closed her eyes, shivering violently.

It had not happened. She hadn't let him do that
to her. She repeated it to herself like a magic
formula which would take away the heat and sting
of the memory. She would have to hate herself if
she had let him...

And that wild crescendo of desire had nothing to do with love! Not the sort of love you built your life on! Patrick was the man she wanted to spend the rest of her life with; that was what mattered, after all, more than anything else.

She went round and round in circles, hour after hour, day after day, getting more and more lost and confused.

It didn't help that she got constant phone calls from Josh, who did not give up simply because she never let him get out more than a few words each time before she hung up. He rang her at least once a day, if not more often, and he came to the flat at odd intervals. She was always afraid he would be waiting when she came home, and would catch her before she could get inside the flat, but her hours were so irregular that Josh never managed to get there at the right time, and she deliberately left for work early and got home late.

She was preoccupied with guilt over Patrick too; she couldn't help feeling that she should confess, tell him what had happened that day in the wood. But every time that thought occurred to her she knew she couldn't. She couldn't bear to. After all, it had only been a moment of madness, so unreal she almost thought she had dreamt it.

Maybe she had, she kept telling herself. Had it happened? There had been something so surreal about those moments: the storm, the wet grass, the wildness that had taken her over.

That had not been her. She couldn't recognise herself in the woman who had been possessed with such terrifying emotions. No, it hadn't happened, she had dreamt it, and it would never happen again; she would never let it happen again.

The next time Josh rang she burst out angrily, 'Why don't you leave me alone? I'm sick of the sound of your voice, and you're making my life a misery!'

'What do you think you're doing to me?' he asked her in a low, hoarse voice. 'I can't think of anything else, my mind's not on my work—Laura, I've got to see you...'

'Go away and stay away!' she almost shouted and heard him groan, a deep, primitive sound that wrenched her stomach.

'I can't, I need you; I keep thinking about making love to you the way I did in the wood...'

'Nothing happened in the wood!'

'Darling, you're talking like a crazy woman. You know it did, and so do I...'

She put the phone down with a dead hand and walked away, tears running down her face.

The only thing she could do to stop herself thinking about Josh was to throw herself into her work, in spite of the difficulty of keeping her mind on it when she was constantly afraid that Josh would turn up either at her home or at work.

The fair at Ransoms was only a few weeks away now; she was busy with the arrangements for it and kept getting anxious calls from Ian Eyre. They met several times at his aunt's home, and Laura liked Lady Flora more each time they met. She came over at first as formidable, autocratic; under that manner was a much warmer, easier woman.

It was from Lady Flora that she heard more about Josh Kern's mother and the story of her marriage, one day over coffee, while they waited for Ian to arrive.

'Nell Kern, my dear?' Lady Flora said when Laura cautiously mentioned the name. 'Oh, yes, I've known her for years; we've been on various charity committees together. A very practical woman, Nell, but warm-hearted, too. She's looking much better lately, I'm glad to see. For years she has been under a considerable strain. Her marriage wasn't a happy one; her husband spent most of his time with another woman, and Nell had to go on living with him, knowing about his affair. I think that sort of arrangement is very stressful. Mind you, when I was young, when divorce was quite out of the question for most people, a woman had to put up with flagrant infidelity and learn to hide how she really felt. But these days divorce is so easy.'

'I wonder why they didn't get a divorce?' probed Laura.

'Nell wouldn't agree to it,' Lady Flora said flatly. 'I think, in the beginning, she hoped the affair would burn out quickly, and later, when she realised it was never going to do that, she had become bitter. By then she and her husband weren't even speaking, I gather. In a way I think her attitude is understandable. She was determined to make sure her son inherited the farm. If there had been a second wife and another family there might have been problems with the estate.' She gave Laura a wry smile. 'And also I think Nell couldn't bear the idea of leaving her home and having the other woman move in there. That would have meant that Josh left, too, of course. He wouldn't stay on there if his mother was forced to leave.'

'No, I suppose not,' Laura said slowly. 'I realise he loves the farm; he would have hated to leave, but I can see he would if his mother left. He's very attached to her, isn't he?'

'He was attached to both his parents, my dear. It must have been very hard for him, all those years when his mother and father didn't speak to each other, especially when he was younger. Such a burden for a boy to carry. I expect it was a tremendous relief to him when his father died last year, and the other woman moved away.'

Laura was moved by the picture of Josh as a boy, living in a house made bleak and embittered by the quarrel between his parents. It must have been a terrible time for him.

Huskily, she said, 'You know that I'm buying the cottage, don't you? Where the other woman lived? I'm afraid Mrs Kern and her son weren't very happy about that. I'd been told something about the past history of the family, but until now I didn't realise just how bitterly they must have resented the idea of the cottage being sold to an outsider.'

Lady Flora gave her another of her dry, ironic smiles. 'That is why I told you all this, my dear. I assure you, I am not normally given to gossiping, especially about one of my oldest friends, but in this case I felt it was time somebody explained to you exactly why the Kerns resented the sale of Fern Cottage. Nell told me that Josh had gone out of his way to be difficult with you, and when you met him here, during that thunderstorm, I certainly felt the tension between you. It was only too obvious.'

Laura's face burnt and she couldn't meet the older woman's eyes. Thank heavens Lady Flora had leapt to the wrong conclusion! At least she hadn't guessed what really happened between them out there in the wood.

Lady Flora was still talking, oblivious to Laura's reactions. 'It's all very unfortunate, but now she's had time to get over the first shock Nell has made up her mind to face the fact that the cottage is no longer part of the estate. Josh, though...well, Josh never gives up on anything. He's very loyal, which is a great virtue, I think, and not so very common these days! But he's also determined to the point of fanaticism, and capable of anything to get what he wants.'

Laura's colour drained away as suddenly as it had risen, and she stared fixedly at Lady Flora, who smiled at her and nodded, as if reassuring her.

'But if you make friends with Nell, I'm sure that Josh will gradually accept the situation,' she promised Laura, then turned her head, her face lighting up at the sound of voices in the hall. 'Ah, here's Ian!'

Laura was grateful for the bustle of Ian's arrival. While Lady Flora was busy greeting her nephew and offering him coffee, neither of them had a chance to notice the frozen look on Laura's face.

Is Josh trying to get me to break off my engagement because then I won't go through with buying the cottage? she was thinking, shock making her icy-cold. It all fitted. The initial hostility, the

threats, the coldness, and then that abrupt volte-
face: the pursuit of her that had begun whenever
he caught her alone. A stream of images flooded
through her mind: memories of Josh kissing her,
touching her, constantly urging her not to marry
Patrick. Oh, my God! she thought with anguish.
It all fits!

Then Ian turned towards her with an expectant
expression. 'Well, any further news on the catering
side? Everything set?'

Laura somehow managed to pull herself together,
put on a bright, phoney smile and start to talk. At
least it kept her from thinking any more about Josh.

When she got back to her flat that evening she
found a letter on the mat from her solicitor telling
her that the purchase of Fern Cottage would be
completed the following week. She dropped the
letter on the kitchen table and made herself a cup
of strong black coffee, then sat down with it, staring
at the letter, her mind in turmoil, remembering the
day when Patrick had brought her an armful of
spring flowers and Mr Dale had rung to say that
he had found them exactly the sort of cottage they
were looking for.

They had been so happy together then. Now,
everything seemed to have gone wrong. She no
longer knew how she really felt about Patrick, only
knew that for weeks she had been possessed by a
terrible desire for Josh which made her hate herself,
turned her life into a nightmare of guilt and shame.

She buried her face in her hands, shuddering.
What am I going to do?

Then, from somewhere deep inside, the old Laura struggled out, impatiently upbraiding her. You know very well what you ought to do! Stop drifting about lost in daydreams, shut Josh Kern out of your head, or your heart, or wherever he has taken over! Get back to work. Start thinking. Refuse to let yourself be possessed like this, by emotions which are like locusts, eating up everything.

She had talked sense to so many friends in the past when they came to her weeping over a lost lover, a broken heart. Surely she could do the same for herself?

She immediately acted on her own advice and rang Patrick's hotel to tell him that before he got home they would own Fern Cottage and could start planning their wedding.

He wasn't there.

'He must be!' Laura protested to the girl on the hotel switchboard. Maybe her English wasn't as good as she said it was! 'Signor Patrick Ogilvie,' she repeated, and began to spell the name.

'*Sì, sì,* I understand perfectly, *signora,*' the other girl said in an offended voice. 'I speak English very good. Signor Ogilvie check out today. He has gone to Florence.'

'Florence?' Laura was dumbfounded. Patrick had left Rome without telling her?

'*Sì, signora.* Florence. Firenze.' The operator began to spell that out for her. Tit for tat! said her voice; that would teach Laura not to be so insulting about people's grasp of languages. Two could spell.

Laura interrupted. 'Do you know which hotel he's gone to in Florence?'

'No,' the girl said with unhidden satisfaction. 'Sorry,' she added, as an afterthought. 'But we do not ask our guests to tell us where they are going when they leave us.'

Laura put the phone down numbly, very pale. She couldn't believe it. Patrick last spoke to her only two days ago. He hadn't said a word to her about moving on!

Had it been a last-minute decision? Or had he simply forgotten to let her know? Why had he left for Florence again? Was this Rae Dunhill going to make him return to every city they had already visited? If she did, this trip might last for months. What was going on between the two of them?

The discovery had overthrown her resolution again, left her knocked for six. She had been clinging to thoughts of Patrick for dear life. But it seemed that, after all, she had nothing to cling to! She was on her own.

A year ago that wouldn't have bothered her at all. She had always thought she was perfectly capable of handling herself, her feelings, her career, her life, without needing anybody else to prop her up, but either she had changed radically or she had never known herself at all, because she was dizzy with uncertainty again.

She sat there for what seemed like hours, trying to decide what she should do now, but she couldn't make up her mind, so she went to have a shower. It might make her feel more cheerful and positive about the situation facing her. Maybe afterwards she would go to bed. Or eat a meal. She wasn't very interested in food, though. Her appetite was birdlike these days; she could never be bothered to eat when she was alone.

As she was towelling her hair in her bedroom a quarter of an hour later, the front doorbell rang. Laura looked at the clock stupidly. Nine o'clock. Who could it be at this time of night? A neighbour wanting to borrow milk or bread? Or maybe that hotel operator had got it wrong and Patrick had flown home instead of going on to Florence?

Laura hurried to the door, barefoot, in her short white towelling robe, and found herself facing Josh.

That was the final straw. She went into a state of pure shock, quite beyond doing what she should have done—slam the door in his face! Not only didn't she shut the door, she didn't even move. She didn't protest angrily at his arrival, tell him to go away and leave her alone, she just stood there staring.

Her eyes ate him up hungrily, and only then did she admit how she had ached to see him for days.

She couldn't see enough of him now, could never see enough of that strong dark face, the eyes like burnished silver, the animal magnetism and powerful grace of that very male body, casually dressed in well-washed blue jeans and a thin black sweater which clung to him like a second skin.

Josh stared back, eyes narrowed, searching, assessing her state of mind, then he calmly walked into the flat, closing the door behind him, while Laura stayed rooted to the spot, trembling, consumed by emotions so intense they paralysed her.

Josh looked down into her dilated green eyes, pushed back the fine, damp strands of blonde hair tangled around her face. 'It seems as if I haven't seen you for a hundred years,' he whispered. 'My God, Laura, I want you so badly... I'm almost sick with wanting you.'

She couldn't have got a word out to save her life. A wild, fierce sweetness was beating through her. She was staring at his mouth and aching for the touch of it.

Josh bent his head, his mouth closed hotly over hers, and Laura groaned, her lips parting, yielding, trembling, her body arching towards him as his arms enclosed her, pulled her closer and closer until their bodies strained together, needing to merge, to absorb each other. He untied her belt, her robe fell open; Josh made a husky sound, his hands reaching inside, restlessly touching her, caressing her damp, naked body.

Laura was burning, dissolving, like a wax candle melting down, lying against him, because she could no longer stand on her own, she needed to lean on him, her arms around his neck, clinging to him, shuddering and moaning with desire and pleasure as they kissed.

Josh suddenly slid his hands down her body, lifted her off her feet, one arm under her knees, the other under her back, and began to carry her towards the bedroom.

She knew where they were going, what would happen, but she no longer wanted to think about reasons or common sense. Her life was out of her own control; instinct was dictating everything she did now. She let herself go with the flow of her own emotions, gazing up at him with huge, dazed eyes, clinging to him, a hand on the back of his neck, another clasping his flushed cheek.

She was aware of nothing but Josh; the rest of the world had faded far away into some remote distance, as if they were on a private planet, but she was conscious of everything about him—his life's blood running fiercely in his veins, the air he breathed, the rapidity of his heartbeat above her own.

The bedroom was shadowy; she had left a lamp switched on by the bed, which was already turned down for the night.

Josh slid her inside the covers, his fingertips brushing her naked body lingeringly, making her heart lurch, her pulses go crazy.

He hurriedly began to strip off his black sweater and she watched, dry-mouthed, as she saw his bare, tanned skin, the breadth of his shoulders, the muscles in his arms, his deep chest and flat stomach.

She was shivering now, icy-cold and feverish all at the same time, as Josh began to unzip his jeans, but before he had pulled them off the doorbell began to ring again.

He froze, staring at her. 'Who the hell is that? Were you expecting someone?'

She shook her head, green eyes dilated, startled out of her tranced mood.

Josh closed the bedroom door. 'We'll ignore them; they'll go away.'

The bell rang again, louder, and whoever it was leaned on the bell this time, so that it rang and rang and rang.

Laura was totally cold now. The fever had subsided. She was feeling sick too. 'I'd better answer it; it might be an emergency,' she whispered, sitting up, the covers held to her chin while she struggled to pull her towelling-robe around her and tie the belt once more. She was not getting out of this bed until she was covered up.

Waves of guilt were sweeping over her. She had so nearly slept with him...another minute and they would have been making love again, the way they had in the woods, with that wild intensity, abandoned to the sheer necessity of having each other. She had told herself it hadn't happened, it had been a dream, a mirage; but it had and she had known that all the time. She had told herself it would never happen again, but she had surrendered as soon as she saw him, without a fight. She hated herself, she hated him.

Josh zipped up his jeans and put on his sweater again. 'Stay there, I'll go,' he said, turning to stride out of the room.

'No! You can't! Whoever it is will wonder...what...what you're doing here...' Laura cried after him, almost falling off the bed.

She had to run to catch up with him, her bare feet making little sound on the carpet, but even then she was too late. Just as she reached him Josh pulled open the front door and Laura stopped dead, her face turning white then crimson, as she saw Patrick outside.

CHAPTER EIGHT

LAURA saw the same shock in Patrick's face as he took in what confronted him. He, too, went pale, staring at her, then he skated a look at Josh, and met eyes that glittered with something between triumph, satisfaction and a sort of pity.

'What the...?' Patrick began hoarsely, then stopped and looked at Laura again as if checking that he wasn't imagining things. He looked her up and down, from her dishevelled hair to her bare feet, absorbing the look of guilt on her face, visibly realising that her body was naked under that short robe.

Laura couldn't meet his eyes. She looked down, but not before she had seen his familiar, smiling features stiffen into a grim mask.

In bitter irony he said, 'I flew back because you said you missed me so much!'

Tears came into Laura's eyes. 'Oh, Patrick...I'm so sorry...'

Josh said curtly, 'You had better come in; we can't discuss this on the doorstep!' He stepped back, holding the door wider.

Patrick turned his angry eyes on him, but made no move to walk into the flat. His voice was thick with pain and contempt. 'There's nothing to discuss, especially with you. It's obvious what's happened and whether it's the first time or has been happening all the time while I've been away, well...I don't want to know the details, thanks. What I do know is enough.'

'Nothing has happened!' Laura broke out, and that was strictly the truth, yet a very partial truth because she and Josh would have slept together if Patrick hadn't arrived when he did, and they had, in the wood, the other day.

Patrick gave her a glance which made her wince. She had known him for a long time, yet never seen him look so hard and remote. All the warmth and charm she had loved about him was gone, stripped from him in an instant, all because of her.

'Are you in love with him?' he asked, and she hesitated.

She had been asking herself that question for weeks, but she still wasn't ready to call what she felt for Josh love.

'I...oh, I don't know...' she stammered, and Josh turned sharply, looked down at her, his silvery eyes fire and ice.

'Don't look at me like that!' Laura muttered, flinching. She didn't know what *he* felt about her, after all! He had never said he was in love with her, only that he wanted her. Oh, yes, he seemed very sure that she was in love with him, but she had never told him she was, had she? So why was he looking at her with that accusation in his eyes? She was caught between the devil and the deep blue sea. Whatever she said, one of them would be furious, and it was Patrick's feelings she cared about. At the very least she owed him an explanation, an apology. She didn't owe Josh anything.

She turned on Josh, her whole body tense. 'Will you please go away and let me talk to Patrick alone?'

His face tightened, and for a second she thought he was going to refuse, but Laura put up her chin defiantly and outfaced him.

Curtly he said, 'I'll wait in the bedroom!' and Laura felt the flinch Patrick gave, and could have hit Josh.

'Go home!' she snapped at him. Her old hostility was back in full force; she felt at that instant that she never wanted to see him again. He had ruined her life: all her carefully arranged plans for the future, her harmonious, tranquil relationship with Patrick. All gone, blown to smithereens by Josh Kern. Her green eyes glittered angrily at him, rejecting him, and Josh stared down at her, then turned on his heel without another word and left.

Laura couldn't meet Patrick's watchful eyes. She held the door open with one hand, the other clutching the lapels of her robe, holding them together.

'Come in,' she said huskily.

Patrick walked past her and went into the sitting-room. She stood in the doorway, feeling very cold suddenly.

'Put the electric fire on, would you?' she muttered to Patrick's rigid back. 'I won't be a minute...'

Then she turned and ran back to her bedroom, hurriedly dressed in jeans and a sweater, before going back to Patrick.

He had put on the fire but not the electric light, so that the room held a warm glow yet was shadowy. Patrick stood by the window, the curtain held back, staring down into the lamp-lit street.

'I'll make some coffee,' Laura said.

Without looking round at her Patrick muttered, 'I could do with something stronger.'

She looked wildly around the room, her mind so distraught that she couldn't remember if she had anything alcoholic in the place. 'I don't think there is anything...you know I don't drink...'

'It doesn't matter; coffee will be fine,' Patrick said, his eyes still fixed on the street below.

She went out and made the coffee, brought it back on a tray, to find him still at the window, still staring out.

'He's down there,' he said roughly, and her heart seemed to stop.

She didn't ask who he meant.

'He's standing on the opposite side of the road, watching me,' Patrick added, then laughed oddly. 'Like a detective in one of those old black and white films. It's started to rain. I hope he gets wet through to the skin!'

Rain wouldn't bother Josh; he was out in the weather winter and summer alike, in thunderstorms or blizzards of whirling white snow; he wouldn't notice a few drops of rain. He hadn't noticed them when they made love in the wood, and neither, she thought in shocked surprise, had she! She sighed. 'The coffee's ready; come and drink it.'

Patrick let the curtain fall and turned away, came over and took his cup from her. Their hands touched; she tensed, quickly drew back, and he looked at her with sadness, reproach in his blue eyes. Laura had never seen Patrick look like this— in all her memories of him he had been cheerfully relaxed. Even his features seemed different tonight: his flesh seemed to have been drawn tightly down over his bone-structure, entirely changing the expression of his face.

What have I done to him? she thought, aching with an affection that hadn't changed, although no doubt Patrick believed it had.

Laura hadn't fallen out of love with him. You couldn't fall out of something you had never been in! It had taken Josh Kern to make her see that her feelings for Patrick were on love's lower key. She simply hadn't understood how much of love was missing from the way she felt about Patrick. She had counted all the ways and been satisfied with being fond of him, liking him, respecting him, enjoying his company. Oh, she could go on forever with all the warm feelings she had had about Patrick, but they still would not add up to one fraction of the emotion Josh Kern had been able to awaken in her.

When Patrick kissed her she liked it, but when Josh kissed her he turned her body to melting fire and knocked down all her defences, left her open to the four winds, vulnerable, helpless. If that was love, then love was more powerful and more dangerous than she had ever realised.

'I was always afraid I'd lose you, you know,' Patrick said quietly, sitting by the fire with his coffee-cup held between his hands.

Laura sat down opposite him, stunned. 'No,' she whispered. 'No, I didn't know...you never gave me the least idea.'

'Well, I wouldn't, would I?' he said, grimacing. 'The last thing I wanted to do was put ideas into your head. You never seemed interested in anyone else, anyway, and when I proposed you accepted, so I grabbed at you with both hands, but I always felt uneasy, never really believed you loved me the way I loved you. I just needed you too much to let you get away, so I hoped I could make myself necessary to you if I really worked at it.' He stopped and laughed humourlessly. 'Maybe I tried too hard! If it isn't there, you can't make it happen.'

Her heart was wrung. 'Oh, Patrick! I feel so guilty, so bad about this...'

He stared into the glow of the fire. 'Oh, I'm not blaming you,' he muttered. 'It was just one of those things. It was what I had been half expecting—that one day you'd meet someone who made you feel the way I felt about you.'

She flinched at that thought. It was true, but she still didn't know precisely what it was she did feel for Josh. She only knew how strong her feelings were, how they had blown through her like a destroying wind, leaving nothing but wreckage behind it.

'I did love you, Patrick,' she protested, and met his eyes, flushing. 'It just wasn't...'

'Enough,' he said tersely. 'No.'

She fell silent. Yes, that was it exactly. What she felt for Patrick simply hadn't been enough. She was amazed at his perception, in fact. He had seen their situation far more clearly than she ever had.

'I shouldn't have gone away for weeks, leaving you alone,' Patrick muttered. 'Although I suppose it was better to find out now than for us to get married only to break up later when you realised you didn't really love me.'

The grief in his voice cut her like a knife and she gave a half-sob. 'Oh, Patrick, I'm sorry...' she began, and Patrick turned his angry stare towards her.

'Don't keep saying that!' His voice was raw. Laura tensed, fear prickling the back of her neck. She had never thought she would ever be afraid of Patrick, and stared at him with incredulous green eyes, her colour coming and going. He watched her, gave a groan. 'No, Laura. Don't look like that. I didn't mean to shout at you. It's just that...well, although I'd always been afraid you'd meet someone else, I can't believe you picked on him...on Kern, of all men! I thought you hated him.'

Her face burned. 'So did I,' she muttered, staring down at her hands clasped around the coffee-cup. 'I think sometimes I still do, and then...oh, Patrick, I'm in such a muddle. I hate him and love him all at the same time; one minute I never want to see him again, and then when I do I...' She stopped, swallowing, and looked up to see him watching her, his face pale and set.

'I can't believe you'll be happy with him, Laura.' He stopped as their eyes met, frowned, burst out, 'No, I'm not saying this because I'm jealous, although I am. I'm serious—I'm worried about you. Be careful, darling. I couldn't bear to see you get hurt, and this man could hurt you badly! Look at the way he behaved over the cottage! The man's some sort of primitive! The two of you have nothing in common; he's not your type at all!'

'I know,' she said, yet inside her a funny little voice was arguing. She no longer knew what her 'type' was, but there were things about Josh she admired. His loyalty and affection towards his mother, his body's strength and grace, his love for his land, the way he seemed to belong to it, as much a part of the landscape as the animals and birds. The more she saw Josh, the more she liked what she saw.

She had so many images of him in her memory now: Josh on his big black horse leaping over the wall and scaring the life out of them that day Patrick first saw the cottage; Josh in his riding coat and boots, his gun over his arm, in the wood, his black hair plastered down with rain, his razor-edged features shining damply; Josh in old clothes, mending a dry-stone wall on a spring morning; Josh looking intensely sexy in his thin sweater and jeans earlier; but, most of all, Josh naked in her bedroom.

Her mouth went dry and her body trembled. She kept her eyes lowered just in case Patrick should catch a glimpse of what was going on inside her. She didn't want to hurt him any more than she already had.

He took a short, audible breath, as if, never-theless, he had somehow picked up on her emotions. 'Well, I'd better be going soon,' he muttered, and, lifting his cup to his mouth, he drank his coffee very quickly, got to his feet, put the cup down on the nearby table and turned towards the door.

'I'll go back to Italy tomorrow. I left Rae in Florence; she was furious with me for suddenly saying I had to fly back to see you.'

'Was she?' Laura gave him a searching look. 'I have wondered if you and Rae were . . . well, you've been talking about her so much, I wondered if there might be something going on between you?'

Patrick began to laugh, stopped dead and looked down at her, shaking his head. 'No, Laura, that was just wishful thinking on your part, I'm afraid. Rae's a friend; we work well together, I'm learning a hell of a lot from her, but there's nothing else between us.' He pulled something out of his pocket and handed it to her. 'This is Rae's latest book; she's signed it for you. There's a photo of her on the back cover.'

Laura turned the book over and stared at the large colour photograph taking up the whole of the back of the jacket.

'Do you really think I'd look at her when I was going to marry you?' asked Patrick drily.

Rae Dunhill had a thin, lively face, with brilliant dark eyes and thick, curly dark hair which was cut rather short, like a boy's. She was deeply tanned and quite striking, but you couldn't call her beautiful, and Laura knew Patrick had always gone out with lovely women.

'Sorry to ruin your hopes for me,' he said with a sarcasm that made her flush. Then he grimaced and gave her a crooked little smile. 'Oh, don't look like that. I'll get over it; we usually do, don't we? Hearts don't actually break, they just acquire a few new scars. In future, though, I'm taking love lightly, the way I did before I met you. You were my big mistake. It's a mistake to care too much.'

She was stricken; what had she done to him? 'Don't let this change you too much, Patrick,' she broke out unhappily, her green eyes wide and glistening with tears. 'I know I've hurt you, but don't make it worse by being like this... You aren't cynical and cold-hearted; don't deliberately make yourself that way because of me.'

He gave her a crooked smile. 'Kind of you to care.'

She winced and he said more gently, 'Look, I'm going to have to protect myself the best I can, Laura, that's all. I don't want any women in my life for the moment, anyway; I've had enough of love. I'll concentrate on my career; I've learnt a hell of a lot in Italy, from Rae. She's a brilliant teacher; she's taught me how to see, for the first time. I had eyes but didn't know how to use them, until I went to Italy with Rae. I think I'm going to move over to Italy to live for a few years, learn all I can.' He broke off, shrugged. 'But you aren't interested in all that.'

'I am!' she protested, and he said with sudden harshness,

'No, darling, don't be kind to me; I couldn't stand that.'

Laura froze, fell silent, her face white.

Gently, Patrick added, 'It will be easier if we end it quickly and cleanly. Could I just ask one favour? Can I come over tomorrow while you're at work and collect up anything of mine around the flat?'

She dumbly nodded.

'I'll leave my key on the kitchen table when I go,' he said with his usual practical eye for detail.

'Thank you,' she whispered, finding this quite unbearable, wishing he would go so that she could break down and cry.

But Patrick was reasserting his calm, sensible nature. 'And if I find anything of yours around my place I'll bring it with me tomorrow,' he said. 'Now, about the cottage; what do you want to do about that?'

That reminded her and she gave a start of shock, realising he didn't know. 'Oh, Patrick, the sale will be completed in a few days' time! I rang to tell you, but you'd left Rome. What shall we do about the cottage?'

Drily he said, 'Well, I imagine Josh Kern has ideas on that subject. He wanted to buy the place back.' Then he frowned sharply and his face changed. 'Laura, I suppose . . . no, nobody would be such a bastard!'

'What?' she asked, feeling very cold and somehow guessing what he meant even before he answered her.

'Nothing...well...just that if Josh Kern wanted the place that desperately he might do anything to get it,' Patrick said gruffly.

Laura half angrily cried out, 'You were right the first time—nobody would be such a bastard! Josh isn't, anyway!' But was she whistling in the dark when she assured herself Josh would never do such a thing?

Patrick nodded. 'Well, you know him better than I do. I hope you're right.' Then he bent, kissed her on the mouth—a brief, deep kiss that made her want to cry again—straightened, gave her one last look, and said, 'Goodbye, Laura,' a huskiness in his voice which made the words sound like a last farewell.

A moment later he was gone, the front door closing quietly behind him, and with that closing door she knew that that part of her life had also closed, as quietly and finally. Patrick would not be back.

But Josh would. She knew that as soon as he saw Patrick leave he would come back up here; and she didn't feel up to coping with him tonight. She was totally drained by all that had happened. She switched off the lights and went to bed.

As she had expected, the doorbell rang as she shut her bedroom door, but Laura ignored it. She took off her clothes again, still ignoring the ringing, the knocking. She had a shower, turning the water on full so as to drown the sound of Josh hammering on the front door.

She towelled herself dry and put on a nightgown, then slid into bed. By then everything was silent. Josh had given up and gone. This time he hadn't even left a note promising to be back. He didn't need to. She knew he would.

She was so tired that she slept the night through. She woke up at seven, in a golden summer morning light, to think bleakly of Patrick, and hope it wouldn't take long for him to get over it. Patrick had never been the brooding, introspective type; he was far too sunny-tempered. But last night . . .

No, she wouldn't think about it any more. There was nothing she could do to change the past; she just had to live with it, whatever her regrets.

She leapt out of bed and went to have a shower, only to realise as she was towelling herself that she still wore Patrick's ring. She took it off slowly, remembering the day he had put it on her finger. She must leave it where he would see it when he came later to collect his things.

When she had dressed she carefully placed the ring on the table in the sitting-room, drank some instant coffee and a slice of toast, and was on her way to the office within half an hour, determined to submerge herself in work.

Josh rang her there during the afternoon, but fortunately she was in a very important meeting and when she saw his name on the list of people who had called her she coolly told her secretary he was never to be put through to her.

Anne's manner was distinctly odd as she nodded, and Laura was puzzled until she caught Anne taking a sideways look at her hand. Then it became clear. Her secretary had noticed the absence of her ring.

Quietly Laura said, 'My engagement is off, by the way,' knowing that sooner or later she would have to explain and might as well get it over with.

Anne's intake of breath ended in a babble. 'Oh...oh, dear...why...what happened?'

'Just one of those things,' Laura said in a flat, cool voice. 'Now, I need the file on the Bennison Trust, Anne—get it for me, would you?'

Anne took the hint, closed her eagerly parted lips and did not ask any of the questions obviously burning on her tongue. She brought Laura the file she wanted and then went back to her own desk, but later in the day, when Laura was about to open the door into Anne's office, she overheard her talking to someone in the room and couldn't help listening.

'No, she didn't say why, she just said it was off; she must be crazy, letting him get away. I think he's simply gorgeous and I'd give my eye-teeth to get a date with him...' There was a silent pause which made Laura realise Anne was talking to someone on the phone, then Anne gave a long sigh.

'Yes, you're probably right; it was probably him who broke it off. I mean, no one in their right mind would want to lose Patrick! I wonder what his new woman's like? She must be fabulous if he's ditched Laura for her. I never thought he would, you know—leave Laura, I mean.' Anne gave a giggle. 'Often wished he would, mind you! Oh, I fancied him rotten, Julia, and so did you, didn't you? Come on, admit it! Yes, I knew you did—we all did, we all hoped he'd notice us one day. He's so good-looking and when he gives you that sweet, little-boy smile you could die for him.' She gave another long sigh. 'And to think we may never see him again!' A pause again, then, 'No, she didn't say. She didn't tell me a thing; you know her—close as an oyster when she likes. She can be so maddening!'

Laura couldn't help smiling at that, but her eyes were wry. It didn't surprise her to hear that Anne had fancied Patrick; that had been obvious for a long time, and, although they had never discussed it, Laura suspected Patrick was perfectly well aware of Anne's feelings because, although he had always been friendly towards her secretary, Laura had often sensed a carefulness in the way he talked to Anne. Patrick was a very gentle man: he wouldn't have wanted to hurt her in any way, or, especially, make her think there was any chance he might stray from Laura to her.

'But if he and Laura have split up obviously he won't be coming to the office any more,' Anne said gloomily. 'I shall miss him horribly, won't you?'

Laura couldn't bear to hear any more. She knew she was going to miss Patrick far more than Anne possibly could. He had been woven inextricably into her life; cutting him out was going to be like having an amputation, because Patrick had been not just a lover, but a friend and a colleague whose work ran hand in hand with her own. The wrench of losing him would leave a vast black hole.

She noisily opened the door and by the time she was in the other office Anne was hastily ringing off. She turned a guilty, nervous smile towards her boss.

'I'm leaving early, Anne, but I'll be calling in on various people on my way home. If Ian Eyre phones, tell him I should be at my flat from six o'clock onwards,' Laura said coolly, and Anne nodded, watching her with those curious, half-pitying eyes as she walked across the room to the other door and out.

That evening Laura half expected to hear from Josh, but he didn't ring, which, although she didn't want to talk to him, made her edgy and started her brooding over what Patrick had said and the chances that he might be right. Had Josh made a dead set at her in the hope of breaking up her engagement? Had his pursuit of her been just an oblique way of getting back his cottage?

She covered her face with her hands, groaning. She couldn't believe it. Josh wasn't cold-blooded enough for that. Ruthless, yes. She knew he was that. Tough, determined, even devious, perhaps— but to set out to break an engagement, ruin someone's life, just to get hold of some property? No, Josh would never do a thing like that.

Ian Eyre rang at eight, just as she was finishing a light salad supper, and talked to her for nearly an hour about various details of the medieval fair. He was having the usual last-minute problems with his designs for the fashion show, and was jittery, but she knew that that happened every time and half teasingly said, 'Stop worrying, Ian; it will be all right on the night!'

'Keep your fingers crossed!' he gloomily said as he rang off, and she promised she would.

Next morning she rang her solicitor to explain the change of plan about the cottage. 'It will be in

my name alone now, not in our joint names,' she
told him. The full purchase price had already been
deposited with him, and it had been Laura who paid
it, using money she had inherited from her uncle a
year ago, so there was no problem about the money,
and the solicitor assured her that the completion
would go ahead on the day arranged.

'I can get the papers retyped with just your name
before then, don't worry!' He paused then said dis-
creetly, 'I'm sorry to hear your plans have been
changed, though. Is there a chance you may get
together again?'

'No,' Laura said flatly, and changed the subject
by asking, 'Would I be safe in giving the builders
their instructions to start work the week after next?
Or should I wait until you let me know the transfer
has been completed?'

'Oh, I don't think there's any risk in giving them
a starting date. If anything interferes with a smooth
completion you can always tell them to cancel, can't
you?'

Laura rang the builder immediately and Alf
Hudson agreed to start work on the cottage in ten
days' time.

'What about the repainting? You never decided
when you would have that done. Summer's the best
time to paint the outside of a house.'

'OK, go ahead and paint it,' Laura said wearily,
not really caring whether it got painted or not. Then
she remembered that Alf Hudson was a friend of
Josh's and burst out, 'I shan't be moving in for a
long time, but you can tell your friend Mr Kern

that I'm not giving up the cottage, whatever he does!'

Alf Hudson sounded startled. 'Oh, aye? Well, miss, I doubt I shall see Josh; he had an accident yesterday and——'

Laura's heart almost seemed to stop. She couldn't breathe for a minute, then she burst out, 'Accident? What happened? Is he badly hurt?'

'I couldn't rightly say, miss. He was riding back from the blacksmith's on that big black mare of his and a lorry backed out of a yard right into them, without any warning! It's wicked the way some folk drive!'

'Oh, no,' Laura breathed, white as a sheet, then asked hoarsely, 'How badly was he hurt?'

'Josh?' Alf Hudson asked, and she could have screamed at his slow-wittedness. Who else could she mean? 'Well, he was thrown, and hit the road at quite a thump, seemingly. Just as well he was wearing a hard hat! If he hadn't been, his head would have been smashed in like an old eggshell. No, it was the horse as came off worst. Ah, in a very bad way, she were. They had to shoot her, and I hear Josh was right upset about that. Almost in tears, they said. He thought a lot of that mare, did Josh.'

'She was a beautiful animal,' Laura said, wincing at the thought of the horse Josh had ridden the day he leapt over her car and scared the life out of her. But Alf still hadn't told her what had happened to Josh, so she huskily said, 'But you didn't say…was Josh hurt badly or not?'

'He'll live, I dare say,' Alf Hudson said cheer-fully. 'They took him to the hospital, so he must have been hurt, and I heard in the pub last night that there was blood all over him when they picked him up from the road, but you can't believe every-thing you've been told, can you? He's as tough as heather roots, is Josh.' Alf Hudson laughed loudly. 'Aye, that's Josh, tough as heather roots,' he re-peated, appreciating his own wit. 'Now, miss, about the repainting of the cottage...had you thought about colours?'

'White,' Laura said absently, not caring a damn what colour he used. 'Just paint it all white, Mr Hudson. I must go, I'm afraid; I'm very busy. Goodbye.'

She hung up, stared at the phone, and then rang Josh Kern's home. A warm Yorkshire voice answered and Laura asked shyly, 'Mrs Kern?'

'Nay, I'm her cleaner. She's out,' said the other woman. 'At the hospital, visiting her son. He's had an accident, riding his horse...'

'Which hospital is he in?' asked Laura before the woman could launch into another version of the story of Josh's accident. She couldn't bear to get a second vague picture; she had to know for sure how badly he was hurt and that meant she had to go there, see for herself.

As she might have guessed, Josh was in hospital in York, a few minutes away from her office. Within a quarter of an hour she was at the hospital; the girl on the reception desk looked Josh's name up and told her which ward he was in. Laura bought a bunch of flowers from the hospital shop and walked for what seemed hours down long, polished corridors smelling of beeswax and disinfectant and the odour of cooking cabbage.

At last she reached the ward she was looking for, and stopped at the sister's office to ask if she could see Josh.

She got an impatient look and a shrug. 'For a few minutes, no longer. He's already had a visitor this morning, and visiting hours are from three to four in the afternoon and from seven till eight in the evening! So please don't stay long. He's at the far end of the ward, in a cubicle of his own.'

Laura was very nervous as she reached the end of the ward. She could see Josh before she got to him, but he was lying back against his banked pillows, headphones clamped on his ears, his eyes shut.

Laura felt her stomach turn over in anxious tenderness at the sight of him, looking oddly younger in his blue striped pyjamas, neatly tucked inside the white sheets and coverlet. She stopped at the end of his bed and stared, absorbing every detail of how he looked. His hair was brushed smoothly down, his face was so pale it seemed to have lost its usual tan overnight, and he had bruises on his forehead, his jaw, his cheeks, the skin yellowish around them where iodine had been dabbed on them; a square piece of sticking-plaster just below one eye held a padded bandage in place. She saw a long, angry red scratch on one hand, and when he shifted in the bed and his pyjama top gaped a little she saw a wide elasticated bandage strapped across his chest.

As he shifted he opened his eyes and saw her. His face went blank, then he scowled, his grey eyes glittering with unmistakable hostility and rage.

'What the hell are you doing here? My God, some women have to have a message hammered home! Look, I don't want you, OK? Just go away and stay away!'

CHAPTER NINE

LAURA was so stricken that without a word she turned round and walked out again, carrying the flowers stiffly like someone going to a funeral. She got back into her car, automatically put the key into the ignition, turned it, then sat there, with the engine running, but the car immobile, staring at nothing, still clutching the flowers while through her head a film ran endlessly. Josh looking at her with apparent loathing, saying in that angry voice, 'I don't want you...go away...'

Well, she had wanted to know how he really felt about her. Now she did. His pursuit had obviously all been a carefully worked-out plan to break up her engagement, stop her and Patrick buying the cottage and moving into it. She had just seen his true feelings in his face, in his voice: Josh didn't even like her and, now that he had achieved his objective and her engagement was off, he no longer needed to bother to pretend.

Laura hadn't known anything could hurt this much. She ran a shaking hand over her eyes, suddenly realising she was crying, remembered the flowers she still held, got out of the car and dumped them into a little bin nearby. A teenage boy in jeans and a gaudy T-shirt who was climbing off a battered motorbike watched her curiously while he took off his helmet. She ignored him; she didn't want him coming over to offer sympathy or ask her questions.

It was only as she drove out of the car park that it dawned on her why he had been so interested. In her driving mirror she caught a glimpse of the boy hurrying over to retrieve the flowers. Grinning triumphantly, he went off towards the hospital carrying them. Laura burst out laughing. It wasn't so much humour as hysteria, and she was very close to tears.

By the time she got home she was silent and depressed. She forced herself to concentrate on work for the rest of the day. She was working on a project for a sales drive by a large department store which had just been drastically remodelled. It should have been easy to come up with ideas, but nothing she worked on had ever been that difficult. She didn't have two ideas to rub together, but she kept trying because it hurt less than thinking about Josh.

A few days later, she finally became the owner of Fern Cottage, a piece of irony she was in no mood to appreciate. She wished now that she had never set eyes on it, and would have put it back on the market immediately if it weren't for her pride and her obstinacy. Any day she expected to hear from Josh or his lawyers, offering to buy the cottage from her, but, of course, she couldn't sell it to him even if she wanted to because the previous owner had insisted that she sign an agreement to that effect, and that agreement was legally binding. Not that Laura would have agreed to sell to him. She would rather burn the place to the ground!

It was a very hot summer day: the streets of York even more crowded than usual with tourists and traffic, the air thick with petrol fumes and noisy with cars and buses. Laura had lunch in a riverside hotel with a client, and when he had left sat on there, too hot and weary to move, staring out of the window at skies which were deep blue and cloudless, while the languorous slow-moving river ran along below the window, fleets of mallard ducks squabbling noisily as they sailed by, a pair of swans drifting lazily behind them, curved necks gracefully bent to sieve the water for morsels of food, hissing at some scantily clad children who suddenly dived into the water near by from the riverbank with shouts of laughter.

Laura watched blankly. She didn't have any further appointments that day, and, since she had no urgent work to do either, she decided not to go back to the office. The city was claustrophobic. She felt as if the ancient walls were closing in on her. There were too many people around, too much noise. She would go crazy if she didn't get away, out of York, into the wide open spaces of the dales, or the moors, breathe fresh air, hear natural sounds—the cry of curlews, the hum of bees on the heather, the rustle of thick green ferns.

Half an hour later, she drove out of the city, without making any decision about a destination, just aimlessly driving through the summer landscape. At first there was heavy traffic, but once she left the main road and drove along narrow, winding country roads she passed far fewer vehicles, and with her window wound right down she could hear larks singing, high above her, like black mobiles suspended from the sky by strings.

Long before she got there, she had admitted to herself that she was going to the cottage, but she had not set out with that in mind. It was a gradual process, a sort of drifting, until at last she found herself close to Castle Howard and knew where she would end up.

As she parked she heard another car close behind her and looked round, as tense as a coiled spring. It wasn't Josh driving the little blue car, however. It was his mother. Nell Kern drew up just in front of Laura's car and got out, smiling.

'Isn't it hot? I went into York, shopping, but I couldn't bear it, so I came home again. When are you moving in, Laura? Let me know, won't you? It's a lot of work, moving into a new home. I'll come and give you a hand, gladly.'

Laura couldn't help the look of surprise, stammering, 'Oh...oh, thank you, that's very kind.'

Nell Kern gave her a quick, searching look, then sighed. 'Look, Laura, we didn't get off on the right foot. I know Josh was difficult with you in the beginning, and I'm sorry. He was doing it for my sake, which isn't much of an excuse, but he knew I was upset about the cottage being sold and that made him angry. Josh doesn't like it when I'm upset. I couldn't have a better son.'

Laura nodded, smiled at her wryly. 'I know. I do understand all that. Lady Flora explained.'

'Did she, now?' Nell Kern flushed a little, but laughed wryly. 'I might have known; Flora's always been the interfering sort. Well, whatever she told you was probably close enough to the truth. But all that's over; I want to forget it, and I want us to be friends.' She held out her hand. 'Can we be friends, Laura?'

Laura took the hand and nodded, smiling tremulously. 'I hope so; I'd like that.' She was confused, though. Nell Kern seemed to be taking it for granted that she was definitely moving into the cottage—hadn't Josh told her that Laura was not now getting married? That he hoped to buy the cottage back after all?

'Have you got time to come in now?' she asked shyly. 'Have a cup of tea with me?'

'That's very kind of you, dear, and I'd love to, but I have to get back. Josh only came home from hospital yesterday; I want to get back to make his tea. But why don't you come back with me?'

Laura flushed and looked aside. 'That's very kind, but I . . . I have things to do here.' She ached to see Josh, but wild horses wouldn't have dragged her to Kern House to face him and see that bitter hostility in his face.

'Oh, well, another time, then!' Nell Kern said comfortably. 'Now, don't forget, dear, let me know when you're moving in and I'll be over to give you a hand.'

She got back into her car, waved and was gone, and Laura walked up the path to the front door and let herself in with the bunch of keys her solicitor had handed her. She walked around the cottage, hearing the strange echoes that seemed to haunt an empty house, remembering the day she had come here to see it for the first time, realising

how long ago it seemed. Those few months had
changed her entire life. She knew she wasn't the
same person who had come here that first time with
Mr Dale. Then her life had been neatly mapped out
in front of her: she would marry Patrick, live in
York all week and come home to the cottage every
weekend. It had seemed a perfect future. Now it
would never happen, and all because of Josh Kern.

She couldn't bear to stay there. The cottage made
her miserable. She walked out, slamming the door
behind her, but as she was unlocking her car she
saw Nell Kern's little car coming back and stared
in surprise, wondering where Mrs Kern was going
now.

Until she realised that Nell wasn't driving it. Josh
was; she saw his black hair, his hard face, his grey
eyes fixed on her as he drove hell for leather, the
car bumping and swaying along the rough track.
Laura's heart turned over violently. She was suddenly terrified. She didn't know what Josh wanted,
but she wasn't staying here to find out. Trembling,
she pulled her car door open and almost fell into
the driver's seat only to see Josh's car flash past
hers, spin sideways and end up with its nose in the
hedge of the cottage, slewed across the narrow
track, totally blocking it and making it impossible
for her to pass him.

Josh was out of the car a second later, just as
Laura got her engine going. She had her window
wide open because of the summer heat. Josh
reached in, cool as you please, and took the ignition key out of the lock. The engine died.

'Give that back!' Laura tried to grab it, but Josh put the key into the back pocket of his jeans, then reached in again and caught her hand, lifted it into the air, stared at it then let it go again.

'So you aren't marrying him!' he muttered, and her colour angrily darkened.

'No. Thanks to you!'

He gave her a narrow look, then pulled open the car door.

Laura shrank back in her seat. 'Don't you touch me!'

Josh took hold of her shoulders and dragged her, struggling, out of the car.

'What do you think you're doing?' she spluttered pointlessly.

Josh gripped her by the waist and the next thing she knew her feet were off the ground and she was being hoisted over his shoulder like a sack of coals.

She kicked her feet wildly into that deep chest, hammering him on the back with her clenched fists.

'Put me down!'

Josh ignored her. He strode through the gate, up the path, to the front door of Fern Cottage which, to her fury, he unlocked and opened with a key he got from his jeans pocket.

'I told you to give that key back! Why have you still got it?'

Josh didn't bother to answer that, either. He walked into the cottage, kicking the door shut behind him.

'Put me down!' Laura said again, but he still didn't obey. Instead, to her deep alarm, he moved towards the stairs. 'Where are you going?' she shakily demanded, and began kicking and pummelling him again, but she might just as well have attacked a pillow for all the effect she had. Josh didn't even seem aware of her feet and hands; he just kept on going and she began to get dizzy, carried head down, over his shoulder, seeing the stairs from such a disorientating angle.

He carried her into the cream and pink bedroom and Laura's heart was beating so hard it was suffocating. Josh stopped beside the bed and Laura found herself sliding down his body, but not to the floor. Josh pushed her backwards on to the bed, then before she could scramble up again he was kneeling on the bed over her, holding her shoulders down against the cream coverlet.

'You can't have the cottage back!' Laura told him fiercely. 'I signed a covenant when I bought it, promising not to resell it to you, so you're wasting your time!'

'Damn the cottage,' he said, and trapped her face between his two hands, staring down into her angry green eyes.

'That's what you've been after all these weeks; don't lie to me,' she told him furiously. 'And once Patrick had seen us together, once you were sure you'd managed to split us up, you stopped pretending, didn't you? When I came to see you in hospital you told me to go away, you didn't want me!'

'Not then,' he said, his mouth indenting, his brows set in a scowl. 'Not while I was feeling like death, and too weak to stand on my own two feet. I didn't want you to see me like that.'

Her ears beat with her quickening blood. 'You sounded as if you hated the sight of me!'

'I had told my mother not to let you know I was in hospital; I told her over and over again that I didn't want you to know anything about the accident. I thought she'd still gone ahead and rung you; she can be as obstinate as you, when she likes,' he muttered. 'That's why I was furious when you walked in.'

'It wasn't her who told me!'

'No, I know; she swore she hadn't broken her word, and she wouldn't lie to me,' he agreed wryly. 'How did you find out?'

'I was talking to Alf Hudson about the work on the cottage and he told me.'

He laughed shortly. 'Alf!'

She nodded, watching him doubtfully. 'Why didn't you want me to know about the accident?'

His mouth twisted in self-derision. 'I just told you! I didn't want your pity! You'd refused to talk to me on the phone or open the door when I came to your flat; I didn't know for sure what had happened between you and Ogilvie, whether your engagement was off or not—but I didn't want you to visit me just because you were sorry for me. I preferred to wait to see you until I was back on my feet and had all my wits about me.'

'So that you could lie about wanting the cottage!'

'I'm not lying about that; the cottage isn't relevant any more, don't you know that?'

Her heart missed a beat. He was staring at her mouth with an intensity that made her tremble.

'I stopped caring about the cottage when I fell in love with you,' he said huskily, and Laura felt as if she had a fever—she was hot and cold all at once, her body trembling. She wanted to believe him so badly that she did not dare.

He smiled crookedly at her. 'I felt guilty about that at first. I was supposed to be blocking the sale of the cottage, for my mother's sake, not falling in love with you.' He grimaced. 'Laura, have you any idea of the sort of lives my mother and I led for years? Ours was a very unhappy home. I love my mother; I bitterly resented what she'd suffered from my father. And then he died. And to my amazement my mother showed every sign of grief—she went around like a ghost, she was always pale, hardly ever spoke, didn't eat. At first I didn't understand, then I realised that she must have loved him all those years, even when he was hurting her so badly. Can you wonder I wanted that woman out of Fern Cottage? I'd have paid anything to get her out, and I didn't want anyone else living here. I had a confused sort of feeling that if I got the cottage back I'd somehow make my mother happier. And then I went and fell in love with you.'

Laura ached with a mixture of hope and pain, wanting to believe him, sick with compassion for him and his mother, sick with love.

'I'm sorry you and your mother had to bear so much grief, Josh,' she whispered. 'It must have been terrible for you, both of you—but I think she's getting over it now, you know, or she says she is...'

'Yes, I know,' he huskily agreed. 'And it's wonderful to see her look so much happier. She looks younger now than she has for years.' And he smiled, his grey eyes tender. 'I suppose time heals everything, and she would have got over it anyway, but it has happened faster because of you...'

'Me?' She looked at him incredulously, and he nodded.

'Yes, she started to look happier after I'd told her I loved you.'

'You told her?' Laura blushed. 'Oh, no!'

His eyes gleamed softly. 'You've gone all pink. Shouldn't I have told her? You don't really mind her knowing, do you?' Then he frowned, and looked uncertain, something Josh rarely did. 'Laura...you do like her, don't you?'

'Very much,' she said at once, in reassurance, feeling tenderness for him and touched by his obvious fondness for his mother. 'Of course I do, Josh. I liked her the minute I met her. But...what on earth must she have thought of me, getting involved with you, when I was engaged to someone else?'

'She was taken aback at first,' Josh admitted, his face wry. 'She's been hurt so much herself that she started worrying about Ogilvie.'

'Yes,' Laura said bleakly, having guessed that that was how Josh's mother would react.

'And she was angry with me for letting myself fall in love with another man's woman,' Josh said bluntly. 'Don't worry, I made it clear that all the pursuing was on my side; she didn't blame you. And she liked you when she met you.'

'It must have been disturbing for her, though, like watching a pattern being repeated,' Laura said slowly, realising for the first time that there was a pattern here, with herself and the two men, a tangled threesome, like Josh's parents and the woman who had lived here at Fern Cottage.

'But this is different!' Josh insisted. 'You weren't married. If you hadn't met me you wouldn't have realised he wasn't the right man for you before you married him, and it would have been much harder to untangle your lives by the time it dawned on you what a mistake you'd made.'

Laura was silent, her face grave. It was true. If she had married Patrick she might have had children who would have got hurt when the marriage broke up, as it probably would have done sooner or later. She had not loved Patrick with the depth and passion a true marriage needed. And yet she could never forgive herself for having hurt Patrick the way she had. A sigh wrenched her and she felt Josh stiffen, frowning.

'He'll find someone else,' he said quickly, reading her mind.

She looked up into his watchful grey eyes. 'I hope so. At the moment he's very unhappy and I hate knowing I did that to him.'

'The trouble is,' Josh said in a low, rough voice, 'love can hurt, either ourselves or other people. My mother loved my father, and he hurt her, and I've never been sure whether he wanted to hurt her or not, whether he ever loved her once, or if he could help himself or not.'

'He didn't have to bring that other woman to Fern Cottage, anyway,' said Laura, thinking about

it and curious about the motives of the dead man.
'That was cruel.'

'I think my mother may have been cruel in refusing him a divorce when he was so much in love
with someone else,' Josh said flatly. 'Maybe she
should have let him go.'

'But she loved him.' Laura looked at him with
passion and knew that she understood completely
why his mother had acted the way she had. 'And
you,' she said. 'She loved you, and she stayed on
for you, so that you could have the farm. She was
afraid if she agreed to a divorce you would never
have Kern House and the land.'

He nodded. 'I know, but I wish to heaven she
hadn't put herself through that for me! Women are
baffling.'

Laura laughed, suddenly finding that funny. 'Not
to ourselves. I think I understand your mother.'

He looked at her through his lashes. 'I think she
understands you; at least I hope she does! When
she came back to the farm just now she told me
she'd seen you and you were no longer wearing an
engagement ring. She said she'd tried to get you to
the farm but you wouldn't come so I'd better go
to you if I really wanted you.' His voice dropped
to a husky whisper. 'So here I am.'

'It's too soon, Josh,' she said, her green eyes dark
with pain. 'I still blame myself for hurting Patrick;
I can't think about anything else yet.'

'You love me, Laura, and you never did love
him,' he said flatly, taking her breath away because
it was so cruelly true although she had only just
begun to admit it to herself.

'I thought I did!' she protested.

'You didn't know what love was!'

Laura was silent, the words ringing in her ears like a funeral bell.

'Until you met me,' he added, and that was true, too. She had not known what love felt like until she met Josh.

'That doesn't absolve me for hurting Patrick!' she whispered, and Josh gave her a strange, sad look.

'You couldn't help hurting Ogilvie once you met me, any more than my father could help hurting my mother once he had met someone he really loved. I didn't plan to fall in love with you, I know you didn't plan to fall in love with me—these things just happen; they're like a sudden avalanche—they just come down on you and bury you and you can't escape.'

She shivered. 'It sounds so grim.'

Josh held her face between his hands, his grey eyes passionate. 'No, Laura. Not grim. Inevitable.' He bent slowly and brushed her quivering mouth with his lips, whispering her name against them. 'Laura, Laura... I'm so much in love with you...'

Her body shook. 'Josh. Oh, Josh...' She put her arms around his neck and clung to him. 'I love you,' she breathed, and her mouth opened under his, the heat building up between them as they kissed.

'Say it again,' he muttered hoarsely. 'I want to hear you say you love me; I seem to have been waiting forever to hear you say it.'

'I love you, I love you,' she said, her body arching closer, shuddering with desire which mounted to her head like the fumes of some strange drug, clouding her brain and making her forget everything but him.

Josh's hands trembled as he began to undress her, kissing her hungrily as he peeled her clothes off.

Laura felt a wild excitement as his hands moved down her body, lingering to caress her naked breast, to fondle the soft curve of her waist and hip, to brush her thighs.

'You're so lovely,' he muttered, bending to kiss her nipples, his tongue warm, tormenting.

Their desire for each other had been the driving force of their relationship; almost from the start she had known in her heart that she wanted him but guilt and distrust and fear had bedevilled their meetings, even that day in the wood when they had taken each other with such passion. This time there was nothing to keep them apart; they were free to love each other, all barriers gone. Laura could scarcely breathe; she was dragging air into her lungs in short, rough gasps, her blood singing in her ears.

She began to undo Josh's shirt, her hands trembling, so hurriedly that she almost wrenched a button off, and Josh started to laugh huskily.

'Careful, darling!' Then he looked down at her and saw the way she looked at him and he stopped smiling, his eyes darkening. He shrugged out of his shirt and stripped off the rest of his clothes while she watched him, breathing audibly, aching with passion for the hard, muscled planes of his body, the smoothly tanned, broad shoulders, the deep chest, with dark hair curling down to his midriff, his strong hips and thighs.

Naked at last, they looked at each other, moving restlessly, with a desire that made them both tremble.

But it wasn't the desire Laura felt that made her love for him so much stronger and more overpowering than the way she had felt about Patrick. Staring at Josh, she knew that now. From their first meeting she had been secretly aware of a fierce attraction towards him, an awareness of his body, a desire for it. But more slowly, under that, a stronger emotion had come into being—not simply love, although she loved him deeply, but something more powerful even than love.

It was sheer need. She had never needed Patrick. She needed Josh in every conceivable way, and she knew with utter certainty that she always would. She smiled quiveringly, aching to express her need, give herself to him and at the same time absorb Josh, taking him into herself, so that they could be one flesh. For the first time she understood the real meaning of those words.

She and Josh were one flesh, one soul: they belonged together as she had never truly belonged to Patrick.

She put her arms around Josh and pulled him down to her. 'I love you,' she groaned, and he echoed the words huskily, passionately.

'I love you.'

POSTCARDS FROM EUROPE

HARLEQUIN PRESENTS®

Hi!

I can't believe that I'm living on Cyprus— home of Aphrodite, the legendary goddess of love—or that I'm suddenly the owner of a five-star hotel.

Nikolaos Konstantin obviously can't quite believe any of it, either!

Love, Emily

Travel across Europe in 1994 with Harlequin Presents. Collect a new Postcards From Europe title each month!

Don't miss
THE TOUCH OF APHRODITE
by Joanna Mansell
Harlequin Presents #1684

Available in September, wherever Harlequin Presents books are sold.

HPPFE9

Harlequin® Historical

LOOK TO THE PAST FOR
FUTURE FUN AND EXCITEMENT!

The past the Harlequin Historical way, that is. 1994 is going to be a banner year for us, so here's a preview of what to expect:

* The continuation of our bigger book program, with titles such as *Across Time* by Nina Beaumont, *Defy the Eagle* by Lynn Bartlett and *Unicorn Bride* by Claire Delacroix.

* A 1994 March Madness promotion featuring four titles by promising new authors Gayle Wilson, Cheryl St. John, Madris Dupree and Emily French.

* Brand-new in-line series: DESTINY'S WOMEN by Merline Lovelace and HIGHLANDER by Ruth Langan; and new chapters in old favorites, such as the SPARHAWK saga by Miranda Jarrett and the WARRIOR series by Margaret Moore.

* *Promised Brides,* an exciting brand-new anthology with stories by Mary Jo Putney, Kristin James and Julie Tetel.

* Our perennial favorite, the Christmas anthology, this year featuring Patricia Gardner Evans, Kathleen Eagle, Elaine Barbieri and Margaret Moore.

Watch for these programs and titles wherever Harlequin Historicals are sold.

HARLEQUIN HISTORICALS…
A TOUCH OF MAGIC!

HHPROM094

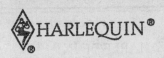